For my brother, Bryan

I Shot Bruce

Brett Busang

Vijay Asunder was apprehended by the police yesterday for assassinating the sole survivor of the most popular singing group of the last century. He said that the wound he inflicted wasn't even comparable to the "festering sores" of rejection, which he has nursed since 1961, when The Keysters let him go in favor of a more polished musician. TV clips from that day show a stunned Asunder leaving the small club where the Keysters were playing.

More news as it happens.

1

*A*nd so it happened. It really did. Jake, Marshall, and Townsend summoned me into a small room that was appointed with a single lampshade, smelled of pongy stuff that previous occupants had left behind, and was illuminated to the point of paranoia. I mean, it looked like the FBI was going to come in with assault rifles. All I remember was shielding my eyes and saying "Shit!" It was as if they had orchestrated the event beforehand and had summoned me there as a *fait accompli*.

"How're you doin', mate?" This from Jake, who was always the consortable one. In subsequent years, he was the band's spokesman, though he put his foot in it now and again. When he said the group had become more popular than the Spanish Premier, he didn't attract a lot of attention, largely because it was said to a French audience—who ate up that sort of thing. But he escalated his "better than's" and went all the way up to the Dalai Lama. Some people didn't think he was overreaching himself, but when the ordinarily even-tempered DL demurred, you knew Jake had committed the gaffe of his career. Sure, he recovered, but he had egg on his face for an entire weekend!

"I'm bleepin' blind," I told him. The other guys laughed, as if I were Oscar Wilde and they Oxford wits down on their luck that morning. It was the morning. The clock said: 11:47. 11:47, my doomsday numbers.

"Adjust the light over there," said Jake, with a rolling assent from all the rest. Hapless Marshall did the deed. He was always doing our dirty-work. No lead guitar for him when he could supply the rhythm for us. Never got to sing anything but harmony, in spite of his warmish tone and cloud-topping soprano. If you want some world-class resentment, read his memoir, *The One Who Carried Water*. If a title had ever summarized a group's tyranny over one man, that one did. When it came out, I wrote him a congratulatory letter. Fucker never did reply. I thought we were simpatico. Guess not.

I muttered a thank you for the adjustment.

"Anything to make you comfortable." This also from Marshall, who was smiling as big as life—something he stopped doing after the band broke up in sixty-nine. But that was the way he was then. He smiled all the time. A lot of people thought him insensitive—even stupid. But he was possessed of an irrepressible love of life. A good chap, straight lad, dyed-in-the-wool humanitarian. If I regret any one thing greater than the rest, it's not being able to take the ride with him. He was great fun to be with. Never down. Some people said he was gay, from all the smiling. We never talked about that, though he did enjoy massaging my shoulders. Said if women liked it, why not the blokes as well?

"Uh, we've summoned you here to tell you something," said Jake.

"What? What Armageddon is upon us?" I asked.

"Nothin' like that," said Townsend, who was truly concerned about what he called my "pessimistic nature." Some of us are made that way. I've always taken a dark view of things. I think it came from the time that my father not only left my mother, but took a little puppy named Sage with him. I still think about that little dog. He would lick me in the face before I awoke in the morning. One time I smacked him clear across the room. But in a minute, his tail was wagging and he was good to go again.

My father came back, but he also died. A wasted bit of business, really.

"We've been talkin' amongst ourselves, y'know, and have come to a sort of..."

"Stalemate." This from Jake, the only one of us with a so-called higher education. Down the road from Oxford he came, quoting Christopher Marlowe and all the other gits.

"That's right. A stalemate."

"But we've come up with a solution," said Marshall again, who was taller than the rest of us. His look alone would have gotten him lead singer in any other band.

"A solution to what?" I asked. I still found the light oppressive, but they'd done all they were going to do.

"This is how it is," said Jake, leaning over to me confidentially. "We've been asked to record a few songs by this curio-sweeper who enjoys his pastries a bit too much, but he seems legit enough."

Everybody chimed in on that one. "Oh, yeah, he's legit to the very core." "No one more legit than Poofy." "As straight as a fence and hard as a rock." Quoth Marshall, who seemed to think that was funny.

"That's great!" I said, little suspecting the trap they'd set for me. I had the pessimist's reverse optimism whereby I was always hoping for something good to happen, but could never quite believe that it would.

"Yeah, it is. It really is," said Townsend. "Yes, it's the thing we've always wanted."

"However," said Jake, looking like someone with a big quote in him. "However, in order for that desired conjunction to occur, that perfect synthesis of talent and opportunity, that ineffable lining up of the stars..."

"Yes," said Townsend, "in order for us to get this contract, well, we've got to let somebody go."

"Oh," I said, already commiserating with that person. (How could I have been so stupid?)

"Yes," said Marshall, who felt that, of the other two, he could deliver bad news with some grace.

"Well, that's too bad. A big break for all, but not one, eh?"

"Yes," said Marshall, who smiled me a big one.

"Well," I said, wiping my brow with a soiled napkin with the club's name on it. "Who is it?"

"I'm afraid," said Jake.

"Yes, it is with profound regret," continued Townsend.

"It's never easy to do these things," hemmed Jake.

"Such a conundrum, you know," hawed Townsend. (Jake looked at him as if he shouldn't be using such a word—that it was his word alone. He was like that. I mean, very possessive of language.)

"One must approach the situation with delicacy," averred Jake.

"And tact as well. Must be tactful—even to a fault!" said Townsend with a concluding flourish. It was now time to state the premise, which, strangely, fell to Marshall, who had the least authority of anyone. Just goes to show you how circumstances make us who we are.

"We've got to let you go," said Marshall, whose smile finally deserted him. His grimness was not of a piece with his smiling nature. It seemed artificial, trumped-up, all wrong.

"What did you say?" I said.

"Jesus," muttered Townsend. "I hate this sorta thing."

"If truth were known," said Jake, "I do also."

Strangely enough, Marshall did not chime in. It was as if he'd suddenly found his medium: the tight-lipped bearer of Bad News.

"You're letting me go?" I asked the three of them.

"*We* aren't, you understand," said Jake.

"No, we aren't indeed!" corroborated Townsend.

Nothing again from Marshall. You've gotta watch an ex-smiler.

"He, uh, Peregrine...Poofy...seems to think that our image needs a bit 'o tweaking."

"That's exactly what he said," put in Townsend. "Tweaking was his very word."

"He believes that chemistry is of inestimable importance in the evolution of any group, be it Aborigines, monkeys in the wild, or rock 'n roll outfits."

"That's exactly right, Jake-O!" said Townsend.

Marshall merely nodded, and less comfortingly than he could have.

"So we had a kind of summit, if you will, in which various permutations of personnel were discussed." Jake seemed to enjoy emitting these rolling syllables, sitting there with his guitar slightly out of tune and his mouth slackening, as if he had said somebody else's lines and was responsible for them only as a third party.

"Yes, that's correct," said Marshall, seeming to snap out of something.

"Incidentally, would you care for a cup of something?" Jake asked me, an executioner before the condemned.

I ran a comb through my hair, which was thinning a bit, but not so you'd notice from the stage, and shook my head. Truth to tell, my stomach was absolutely in knots. If I were by myself, I'd probably care to void it.

A girl came in, one of those birdy creatures with straight blond hair, legs that seemed twice as long as they were, and lips that pursed like no librarian.

"Sorry," she said. "Didn't know you were in a confab."

"Perfectly all right, Mother Teresa," said Jake.

"Want anything, gents?" she asked, shaking her bottom—though I don't think *she* shook it. It shook all by itself. She was wearing something that wouldn't be popular for some time: bell bottoms. And her stripy blouse covered her like a second skin, which showed her bosom to great advantage. This was the day when a great body was shaped as much by the things underneath as by its born-with stuff. Imagine, if you will, a bosom that stuck out at right angles to the rest of her and you'll get an idea of the impression she made. Her skin was of a tawny hue that reminded me of all of the colors one missed here in London. It suggested tropical fevers, muted sunsets, and careening desires—though I will admit that my views about her were subjective, as were everybody else's. There was something about her gait as well. It seemed to be made up of separate motions, which, for a split second, operated independently, as in a photograph of a running horse. The hips swiveled; the ankles pushed up; and the bottom rose to meet them. All eyes followed her, including mine. She was a knockout then and nearly a knockout today, though all the plastic surgery is beginning to show. She'll be giving an interview and her lips seem to form the words long after they come out. Then as now, you looked at those lips and imagined what they could do. She was about our age, but had a more worldly demeanor to her. Jake married her for a while, then Townsend. Then Jake again. She made a lotta money off of that second time. And wrote a book in which she postulated that not only was Townsend gay, the whole lot of them were. She claimed to have pictures, but never produced them. Yet her word for the group—inseparable—stuck. It was always the "Inseparable Jake and Townsend", the "Inseparable Keysters", and so on. I started to find it morbidly ironic considering my outcast state. And I never ceased to think of it that way. It is as ironic now as it was then. Some things just last, y'know?

"Let me get this straight," I said, rising from my chair. I dropped my comb, then a set of keys, then something else, thereby compromising a dignity that was never my strong suit. It seems like clumsy people never make their way in the world, unless they make a comedy routine of it.

"It's not the way we'd want it," said Townsend.

"Not really," said Marshall, whom I wanted to believe, but didn't.

"You see..." said Jake, picking up my keys for me and jangling them a bit. He didn't finish his sentence because he found himself, as his many biographies explain, having a "eureka" moment.

"Hmmm," he said, "that reminds me of something." And went over to scrawl a few words on a paper napkin. He would later claim that my drumming-out was the genesis of "Finster Boy", which was one of the first rock songs to use a full orchestra. I'll have to say that, even if I were ill-used on that day, the song is really powerful. There was a boys choir in it. And some eerie violin-scrapings. They send a chill down my spine to this day. But I hated the chorus then and I hate it even more now, when subtext is so much more obvious than it was at the time.

> *Oh, Finster's coming home*
> *Yes, he will never roam*
> *Again!*
> *Oh, Finster, he's got no pride*
> *But anybody with a grand illusion*
> *Does all right in the end!*

I hate that song because it's about my downfall, but I like it as a work of art—if you know what I mean.

"The boy genius!" said Townsend, as if Jake was one of those bad little blokes you like to reward with some extra rashers when nobody else has anything.

"You're sacking me. Right here in this smelly little room. You're sacking me, aren't you?"

"Well," said Townsend.

"Sorry, old boy," said Jake.

"Yes, I'm afraid we are," was Marshall's comment, which he made without flinching.

I can't remember whether I fainted or not, but I lost consciousness the way a swimmer does when he swallows too much water. And if there's nobody around, he swallows more than a body can stand. I was lucky, wasn't I? I had three good friends around to prop me up and stuff money in my pocket.

Yeah, good friends indeed...

It was past twelve. But my doomsday calendar began at 11:47—a time I won't forget for as long as I live.

2

*W*hen life serves you lemons, what do you do but suck on them like a sixty-year old whore? That doesn't mean that, like that superannuated expert, you wouldn't spit them out. Or deny that the lemons had puckered your face to begin with. You're not necessarily born with a philosophical attitude, but life's vicissitudes can make it grow. I think that's why a lot of successful people seem one-dimensional. It's life's lemons that promote philosophical reflection. When you are among The Chosen, you get the biggest apples in the basket. It's all nectar and no cavities. And, when it isn't, you can look back on all of those succulent creations and remember what they felt like in your hands; hear the vacuous chomp; pucker disingenuously; and wipe the sugary drool from your chin. Yet I wouldn't have minded risking a one-dimensional personality if it were teamed with one-dimensional perks and privileges. Just as all of us might be murderers, the surly servant could jump into a plutocrat's trousers and like strutting around in them. Our principles happen according to what happens to us. If we double-fault all the time, we become depressives—or comedians.

But we do not win.

I have some recollection of what happened afterwards. There in that smelly room, all by myself. A single light burning and some distant moving about. Boxes or something. A sliding sound. Hiss hiss hiss.

I decided I'd get up and go home.

"Oh, it's you!" said the manager, one Fitzwilliam Moultrie, who liked to dally with rock 'n roll because it was at such a remove from his day-job as a department store maven.

"Yeah? And what of it?"

"That ineffable working-class rage! I love it!"

"Just get out of my way," I said, like the cowboy who will bluster into those double-doors that lead to barroom brawls and smashed-up chandeliers.

"Temperament leads the way—yes, in one art form after another!" he exclaimed with a flourish.

I'd guess he was one of Peregrine's friends. What was it about us that attracted so many boy-lovers and bum-hole guys? I guess it was the excitement of a New Thing. Well, I wasn't about to be his fantasy and got the hell out of there.

The bird I mentioned was sitting near the bar, reading. In those days, girls read stuff. It was cool and sexy, particularly if you were sexy already. Somehow a sexy girl with a book in her hand became exponentially sexier. At least *she* did.

"You looking for your lost comrades?" she asked me.

"No, not really," I said. "I think I just need to go home."

"See you tomorrow, then."

"Right. Tomorrow, tomorrow, tomorrow..."

I'll admit that I wasn't above cheap histrionics.

I was living with me mum at the time, in a flat near Picadilly. She was always miffed when I came in late.

"Is it you?" she asked me from outside the door. "I thought it was the night watchman."

"There are no night watchmen," I said, truly enough. She was a real Englishwoman impersonating a real Englishwoman who was acting in an English movie. I tried to explain that concept to her, but it only made her mad.

"If you don't mind, I'm goin' up to me room," I said.

"I don't mind. Don't worry about me. I've just been waiting up all night, that's all."

"I'm sorry, Mum. Had a rough evening."

I turned to go upstairs to my boyhood room. I'm not ashamed to say that I still lived there. I knew it would be temporary, as long as I was with the Keysters. Oh, yes. I knew they were going somewhere. And they were right, insofar as it goes, about chemistry. Or Peregrine was. They really did need the right combination of temperaments and personalities, the kind of "Oh, yeah!" effect on people they would eventually have without me. But let me tell you: we did all right when I was there on the bandstand, shaking a tambourine, blowing on a mouth organ, or just swinging with the groove. There are pictures of me doing that and I looked not so much like a young Adonis, plugging it out by myself, but a perfect little cog in a wheel. People shouldn't knock second bananas. They make the top ones stick to the tree.

"Oh, that's all right. You'll just have to let your mum worry about you."

"I know, Mum," I said and kissed her on the forehead, which was dry as a churchman's wallet. I lost my dad—and she, her husband—way back when I was thirteen. Hit by a lorry. Killed so instantly that he had no last word, or words. Entered through the back door of eternity with a cup of petrol in his hand. The driver was so sorry that he went nearly mad. Me mum said I should go to his flat and forgive him. Right then. So many years later.

"Why now? After all these years?"

"Better safe than sorry," she said in that self-righteous, head-tilted-toward-the - h e a v e n s, eyes-cast-lower-down standing-on-perfectly-flat-feet sort of way. It was as if she'd rehearsed the wrong play, but did it so well that one had to go along.

"Look, I've got troubles of me own. This very evening..."

I started to moon about it, but she mooned me one better.

"All right. If you don't want to, that's your prerogative—it's one's privilege to hold his tongue, even when the innocent may suffer. Yes, it is one's privilege to do that."

She gave me a perfect I'm-being-abnormally-fair-to-you smile, composed of anger, self-love, and, strangely, genuine forgiveness. When all's said and done, she had become, after there was no more Dad, a good woman—if not the lady she probably wished she had, at some point, aspired to be.

"Let me get this straight. Almost ten years after the fact, you want me to run to some tired bloke's little flat and tell him...what is it you want me to tell him?"

I'd lit a cigarette and snuffed it out on the table where she put the mail. She ran reproving fingers over the ash, which sprinkled, like fairy dust, to the floor. I coughed as if I'd taken too deep a drag and struck a sulky pose. The mirror told me how effective it was, though it would have been more effective with the cig—a kind of penile extension into an obscene No-Man's-Land—projecting from my lower lip. A place neither here nor there; betwixt or between. A perfect limbo. Desire is acceptable only in the desirable. In everyone else, we shirk away from its *moues* and manifestations.

"That, after considering the, the ramifications of what he did....the fact that he was innocent in God's eyes...and your own personal qualities...that you forgive the man his transgression and absolve him of the guilt that must still be festering within him."

Watching myself and regretting that, from then on, I'd be doing it alone, I felt horribly aggrieved. And put upon.

And royally—yes, royally!—peeved. I put my sulking into overdrive, asking myself why I couldn't have done that earlier—it might've swayed the band-members into a provisional settlement. I would've been cast aside temporarily. Or given a chance to redeem myself. Or been the benign victim of a hoax that could not, in all decency, be maintained.

"For killing Dad? No, I'm not doing it," I said, suddenly finding the request obnoxious, but not necessarily out-of-synch with time as we knew it. Did we know it? On that day, I was aware only of the time on that clock. The rest seemed blurry, a sort of peripheral signature around which everybody else fox-trotted to some signature of their own. I guess what I'm saying is that not only was time slowed down, it was present—palpably so. As if the minute hand had jumped away from its orbit and was darting about on its own.

"You must," she said, taking my face in her hands. "You must for the sake of your...your...I'm losing the word. Karma! You must do it for your karma, and everybody else's too."

Even as I was sticking my chin out, I wondered about karma.

"And karma *is*?" I asked in that hostile way of people who really don't care for an answer. The Valley Girl perfected it some years later. I was working without a blueprint.

"It's something where you attract everything that's coming to you through how you behave. So if you act right, good things will come to you. I've been trying it, and you know, I think it's working. I found a half-pound note on the sidewalk. Up to now, I've just been taking in spare change. A half-pound note! That's what karma does!"

Her theology was not subtle, but it had a sort of practicality, which always makes sense when you're (as the song says) down and out.

"All right. I'll go to him," I said, looking at my hair,

which was disheveled, but appealingly so. I started to lose it at seventeen. At thirty, I looked like a barrister in a bad job. I mean, without the wig.

Image. It's everything in an entertainment career, but, as I've found out, lo, these many years, it means a whole lot less when lights are low, the ale's hitting you just right, and you have money in your shirt pocket.

3

I went over to talk to the sad bloke who'd run over my dad.

To do it, I had to walk over to Kensington, where his flat was located. Nice place—and appointed like a small parsonage. Curtains with flower patterns that calmed the nerves, a sturdy sofa, and a good wife who was a little more than friendly.

"Glad you could come," she said, ushering me inside. As she removed my jacket, she seemed not to want to hang it up. I watched her with it for a moment and it embarrassed me. It had come alive for her, even though I wasn't in it. It was among my first glimpses of the harrowingly secret lives of adult men and women.

I was wondering, in the back of my mind, why Mum had arranged it then. Had she been mulling over what to do all these years? I'm inclined to think that it was one of her impulses. She'd probably read a novel about redemption at the hands of forgiveness (or some such) and wanted me to play one of the parts. When I got home, I could tell her all about it: from a chilly reception to a smashing *denouement*—with which Little Nell got you back in the day. Since Dad had left us, she'd applied for the "spunk" (hate that word!) she'd been missing, and got some of it back. She was no longer rough with things in the kitchen; the breakfast crockery was whole, and her attitude—particularly in the morning—could almost be described as sunny. She even had lunatic ideas about the brotherhood of man, which was coming to all of us, a smiley-faced Apocalypse arranged by Walt Disney himself. She would mutter suggestively about End Times followed by an Era of Grace and Prosperity. I'd tell her that she was dreaming—as she most certainly was. But she was so serenely convinced that I couldn't move her. She'd go up to her room wearing a secret smile on top of a soiled apron. Jake could have written a song about her. And almost did. Bruce's *Day At Lourdes* came pretty close, though the lady he'd chosen was clearly bonkers. It did, however, show off Townsend's guitar, which steadied it with a relentless dum-de-dum, dum-de-dum. I heard it on the Tube not long ago. Guy was listening through an old Walkman, which he'd turned up so that his ears would cease to register non-electronic sounds. I got the words, but it was those dum-de-dums that alerted me to a Keyster Moment. Dum-de-dum, dum-de-dum, then Bruce singing about a lonely old bat who wore herself out making pilgrimages from Brighton all the way over to France. Over and over. As if one day's salvation could only keep her overnight.

> *When you're down, you begin to see*
> *That I'm not you and you're not me.*
> *No, it's just you, my friend*
> *Facing the end*
> *And hoping foolishly.*
> *But what else can one do?*
> *You are forever you*
> *So why not—oh, why not?—begin?*
> *Yes, why not—or why can't you?—begin?*

Yeah. It was Townsend's drum-beat without any drums. (Marshall did his manual one-step, which was neither lustrous nor obtrusive.) No one had ever sounded like Townsend, and is not likely to again.

I should mention that I'd gone to a little pub beforehand. Nice place. Had all the "in" groups on the walls, plus snappy-looking pictures of James Joyce—for a bit of Irish subversion—and Harry Lauder, which appealed to the older types. I ordered two drafts and drank them right down. Then two more, after which the bartender, with a cautionary look, alerted me to the possibility that I had the chucking-out potential of which he was acutely aware.

"I think that's your limit," he said to me, with the insulting knowingness of his kind.

"I'm glad to have your thoughts. What if I order another and attempt to derail your premise?"

I was at my defiant best: arms akimbo —though I don't quite remember how I confronted him—chin out, hair in more or less supportive unrest. Some older patrons were throwing darts behind me. I could feel them whizz from wistful fingertips to the soft tissues of the board.

"All right with me. Just giving you your warning."

"I appreciate your courtesy," I said, hoping he'd add more to it.

"You from around here?" he asked, in order to keep me talking.

"If, by 'around here', you mean the City of London, I plead guilty to that assessment."

"I was just thinking that you might be a figure to be reckoned with on the pop scene. I noticed, the moment you sat down, the aplomb that comes with people who entertain other people. And do all right at it."

Another poofter? I could handle him.

"I'm not in the entertainment business. I happen to be a liaison for a party who takes a keen interest in sheep."

"That's interesting," he said, with a tentative erasure of the skepticism which is epidemic—as it probably should be—among barkeeps.

"No, it isn't. Don't humor me."

He turned to me with one of the most cheerfully pitiless smiles I have ever seen.

"I'm not. You're clearly a man of vision. Of artistic integrity. A man whom fate has wronged and the world keeps under its foot like...like a cinder."

Being in my cups somewhat, I responded to this shred of sympathy without sparing much of that quantity on my interrogator/friend.

"What would you know about vision?" I asked him. Then I had to raise the bar: "Vision is a deeply personal matter. I mean, some people have it and some don't. I mean, I'd like someone to tell me why one vision must predominate and another vision is cast aside. Could they tell me with...with a certain logical precision...about the failure of one vision and the triumph of another. That is all I care to know before I confront a dastardly killer—a man so unscrupulous (is unscrupulous the word?)—that he could plough into an innocent human being. An unoffending human being. And kill him. Therein lies the pitfalls of, I don't know, a vision deficit. Yes. A vision deficit. That is at the heart of what I'm talking about."

The bartender said something about getting me another, at which point I decided I should leave. I passed all of the photos of the patrons, the spit-polished bar, and the cigarette burns on the tables, and I got the hell out of there. I sobered up in record time and wonder why to this day. Perhaps when you confront the murderer of your father, you must be aware. You must become the best possible version of yourself anyone has, in this world and the next, ever seen. But that wasn't the half of it. Dad was hardly on my mind at all.

In those days, I walked a lot. Too restless to take public transportation. And, sometimes, nothing in my pocket to make an easy rider of me anyway. So I jostled around various storefronts, pausing, in random fashion, between a glass trinket or spool of sausage. One window sported a poster of its coming attractions: a band called "The Seven Kippers" and a lady singer with scowl-ready lips and hair that looked somewhat like the actress who played the Addams' Family matriarch (which I didn't catch until after it was popular in the U. S.) on TV. I studied her for a moment and realized that I might not have her, or anybody like her, anymore. And I ripped the poster down with the sour satisfaction that comes to every loser since time began. It gave me such a disappointing little shiver that I thought I might pin it back up. But I left it on the pavement, along with some butcher paper that had blown alongside it. As I kicked it away, some blood came up. That's civilization for you. A bit of a crude veneer, with death puddling up behind it.

At a corner, I thought I'd play Russian Roulette and not look both, or any, way and started walking. Sure enough, a tub-shaped thing swerved to avoid me. I really don't know how he, the driver, did it. I looked up into headlights that were as big as a house and was spared the fate of so many other people who had looked into a battery-powered eternity and paid the price. When it was on its way, I even pinched myself, like a bad actor would in a movie. I looked toward the car, which had slowed down, not so much to see if I was all right, but to shoot me a look. True to the Englishman's nature then as now, there was no obscene gesture, just a small man. A small man looking through the rear window. His face seemed to say: *don't go getting yourself killed. It isn't worth it. And, besides, you'll cause a lot of trouble that way.*

Which reminded me of my errand. Wouldn't that have been ironic, to have offed myself on the way to make amends with my father's killer? Very neat and tidy! Son is run over before he can say the words that'll make everything all right! That's the word: *ironic.* And a story to beat the band with. Yes, to beat the band indeed!

When I got to the address, I felt like smoking, but had left my cigs on the table where the ashes were. Where the mail used to be. A quite serviceable little thing, on the miniature side of most things I'd grown up with. Miniature books. Miniature gas-ring. And miniature notions about honor, dignity, and the triumph of native values.

The place was as unassuming as most of the others: Industrial-age brick held together by a string of mortar, gloomy-looking ironwork, and some garish stained glass, into which the number of the street was etched. The war had shaken its timbers—or, rather, shivered them—but the patches seemed to enrich its character, which had never been full-blown. Just a little house for little people who had, in this case, invited tragedy into their lives in a sudden and appalling way. And here I was, almost ten years after the fact, half-snockered and hostile as a *maître 'd* with a bad night already in him, impersonating an angel of mercy. An angel of mercy with skin-tight slacks, a ducktail roaming around his head, and a vial of resentment churning inside of him. Before I knocked, I wondered if I might just exit the scene right then, when it was still perfect—no, stillborn. But I knocked because I might as well just get it done. I'd catch so much hell from me mum—the hell of averted faces and overblown politeness—that defection wasn't, now or ever, worth it. And, besides, I needed more distraction than I'd gotten from that bartender.

Then the door swung open and I was inside. Smelled like bad coffee, lard left out in a tin, and the kind of shoe polish that stays moldering in an old rag.

There was some old-fashioned stuff on the victrola. Stuff I never liked. Brass band, pace like an old man preparing for dinner, and a lady in a svelte gown singing about the moon. The music was as dull as the patterned dress and the bouffanty hairdo. Yet under that dress, I'll bet it was nice and soft, so you can't judge people by their exterior. Well, you can, but it's not as important if you're likely to get beyond it.

"He's waiting for you," she told me, then gave me a little push. I was startled by it. Full on the buttocks, then off you go.

I saw his head first, resting on the back of a small chair. He was reading his paper, or pretending to. Fire at a school for the deaf. Good prices on shirts and collars.

He didn't address me until I was standing right in front of him. There I was, standing; and there he was, sitting. I couldn't tell who had the upper hand.

I was glad for the distraction. I was feeling low about the incident I have hopefully not described at unseemly length.

"Care to sit down?" he asked me. His voice was softly reassuring. Not like a murderer at all.

"Uh...no, I'll stand."

"I don't suppose you'll forgive me because, if I were in your position, I probably wouldn't forgive me, but I want to say that I'm deeply sorry and, if there's anything I can do for you, I wish you would name it. And if it didn't involve climbing up the Eiffel Tower or shooting a policeman, I'd try to be up for it."

It was as if he'd just done it. Sat there in his chair re-imagining it over and over. And here I'd taken my time— to the tune of...how many years? It was as if I'd intruded on a thought process that was ironclad and didn't need me to keep it going. Yet its intensity was electrifying. Watching him there in his accustomed sense of shame made me feel like a poor pupil—the sort of git who muffs his assignments and makes his teachers take it personally.

"That's all right," I said, "You don't have to do anything."

He shifted in his chair, revealing more of himself. His was not a prepossessing figure. It was almost sticklike in its austerity. Looked like he was on an ascetic diet. Water and crusts, with a smear of something white.

"Why don't you try to think of something? I'll never be more ready than I am now. I mean, I've done everything I can to atone, to expiate, to make amends. But I want to do something for you personally. Please think of something! Oh, please!"

The man he killed wouldn't have abased himself so much, but at least he, his murderer, was sincere. So I thought about it for a moment and said he could go to a little club called the Dead Falcon and he could jeer and ridicule the band there.

"I beg your pardon?" he asked, slightly stricken. If I weren't there, he might've asked his wife to bring him something. Hell, he might've keeled over in his chair. What we don't know about the private lives of other people could not only fill volumes, it would stagger our mundane imaginations. A man calls another man and says hello. After forty years. How hard was that? Can it be measured by the usual algorithms? I'd say not, but what do I know?

"Just make a small spectacle of yourself." I was saying. "The whole point is to put the band in a bad light."

He made an open-handed gesture, as if to ask me where on the moon was I presently living? I ignored it and kept going.

"You'll want to know when. We, or rather they, go on at seven o'clock and play all the way through ten. Show up anytime and, well, go at them. Just say any objectionable thing that pops into your head. And make sure it's directed at the band. They're called The Keysters. There's three of them unless they've gotten a fourth already, goddamned them!"

Then, of all things, I started to bawl.

"There, there, young man. Let it out. It'll do you some good."

"They didn't want me!" I exclaimed. "Me! I was the fulcrum of that unit. I was its nerve center. I was the straw that stirred the drink!"

"Yes, just let it out. I was like that for a while.

Uncontrollable. Just sat here and wept all night. For a while, I was on a suicide watch."

I went to the far corner of the room, sank to my knees, and beseeched an indifferent god or goddess.

"Why wasn't I good enough? Or smart enough? Whatever I wasn't? Whatever that fruitcake didn't see in me, I wish I was that. Oh, how I wish it!"

The old man came over to me, but after a moment, withdrew. "You're not talking about your father at all."

"More than life, I wish I was still in that band!"

He withdrew some more. She came in and stood behind him. They looked like a perfect waxworks, the two of them stock-still and me thrashing about epileptically.

He put a protective arm around her—something he probably didn't expect to do that evening. You can always tell when couples are done with sex. Or wanting to be. Or hoping it would be consumed by something else. He wanted it, but she didn't, which isn't always the case at their age.

"They didn't think I could cut the mustard. Well, I'll show them. I'll join another band—a better band!—and we'll twist and shout and frug their arses off. They're not so good. And, I mean...I mean, what are the odds of them making it out of a stupid little club into the wide, wide world? Everybody's trying to do that, and they don't have any more of a clue than anybody else. We're all just groping about with blinders on, like pigs in a wallow, and we don't know any more about what's going to click than Jesus did when he started that little thing called Christianity. Admit it, you two. Does turning the other cheek really appeal to you? Do you love thy neighbor over there, refrain from coveting his wife—or, in your case, Miss, her husband? And what's this about brotherly love? It's a cutthroat world out there and each and every one of us knows where the jugular is. It just so happens that we haven't had the opportunity—or the blade-strength —to reach it. Come on. Tell me how *you* pick a winner. You don't know any more than I do."

I faced them like a prophet who was clearly running out of steam. Their faces had a porridgy look, scrambled together as one, and looking out from the depths of their startled souls.

"But *I* do. I know these people are going to make it. I knew it last night, when they called me into that smelly room and revealed their plan, which was to strike into the future without me. That was not a life experience, but a totally dead one. I feel dead, that's what I feel like. I may never live again. No, I may never know what it feels like to draw breath without this thing looming over me. No, I don't think I will."

I went over to the man who had killed my father and looked into his eyes, which were more or less kindly. His wife had withdrawn a little, as ordinary women, when faced with lunacy, always do. But they were both curious about me. Something strange had come into their lives and they were fascinated by it.

"I'm sorry to have erupted like that," I said.

"That's all right," he said, though the words seemed to be somebody else's. He was living, for now, through his eyes, which seemed permanently startled.

"We all get into moods," she assured me, withdrawing a bit more into their gassy rooms.

"And, sir, you don't have to go to the Drunken Parrot..."

"Dead Falcon," he said.

"What? Oh, yes. Falcon. I get the two confused. Birds of a feather, y'know. Anyhow, you don't have to go there for me and harass those people. I can do it myself. No, I won't do that. I won't give them the satisfaction. I'll go home and resume life as if they never happened."

"I'm sorry about your father," said the man. The woman nodded her assent as if she couldn't bear to be left out.

"Yeah. He was a good man. But you know what? Good

isn't good enough. I'm sorry to say that, but it isn't. It just isn't."

I showed myself out the door and went to the club, where I stood outside and watched people go in and out, though mostly in. The neon seemed brighter, the crowds more enthusiastic. And they had chosen the "other one." His name was Bruce. I mean, what kind of a name was that? You had Jake, with its jaunty quality; Townsend, which was tony; Marshall, which reminded you of the Marshall Plan. And then there was Bruce. He'd never last a week. Bruce. What a frightful name, like something you pull out of the world's stupidest lottery. A lottery for stupid people only. Conceived by the stupid, played by the stupid, and won by a stupid man or woman nobody would ever hear from until they spent the goddamned money and needed a goddamned roof over their heads.

4

I can't tell you how many times I've played that incident in my head. It's the bellwether experience people talk about in wartime. The bombs are coming down, bullets ping off stony facades, and yet there's a calm and clarity that give hope and meaning to the rest of one's life—no matter how stupidly trivial it comes to be. You always have that, and you can always replay it. Well, the night the other shoe dropped is what I still play in my head. Oh, I've moved on and have cultivated a genial exterior. At every significant anniversary, the radio people interviewed me and asked whether I might be just a tad bitter. I always told them no, not a bit of it. The chips fell where they would, and I went me own way. Bruce went to the Caucasus and almost fell to his death; Bruce became the international heart-throb who could have fornicated non-stop if he and the others weren't making records; yes, Bruce was the dreamy-eyed ingénue the girls swooned over more than the rest. Though he was clearly gay. I mean, even I could tell that. His greatest song is so gay you almost have to toss frou-frou around it. Assuming it wasn't there all the time.

I wander, could there have been a pause
Some lingering applause
As he slipped out of the door?
No footsteps on the floor
Just an extraordinary roar
In my head.
Yes, inside of my head!

Come on, people. Even Jake couldn't defend him when he went off to the Galapagos, presumably to save some turtles, but not without his favorite "guardsman", as the press would call the man. I mean, really! I realize that Bruce's animal activism was sincere, but so was his affection, as it were, for "the man."

After I re-gained some emotional equilibrium, I went, in a small way, into the antique business—for which I had a knack I couldn't have anticipated. And until the other day, I did pretty well at it. I was one of those guys who would appear in a provincial version of the Antiques Roadshow, appraising a bit of silver, mooning over old porcelain, or inducing heart failure in a shy old lady when I announced, with as many dramatic pauses as I could get away with, that her greengrocer painting was worth six thousand quid. Occasionally, though, someone would ask me if I was the Vijay Asunder, the Keyster Might-Have-Been, and the world would stop on its bloody axis. There's basement footage of me fielding questions—having become an antique myself—from an American airhead who had just enough savvy to make me want to kill her. It morphed, for a short period of time, into an international sensation. If it had happened now, you could say it went "viral". As it is, one may see as many bootlegged videos as one cares to; they're all over the Internet. But you, dear reader, are not obliged, because I can visualize the whole thing.

"I couldn't help but notice your name," she said, American perkiness vying with a major thyroid problem to make this woman look like a two-legged Pekinese. A fat, two-legged Pekinese.

"Yes. It is Indian, though I was never in the country where it, my name, originated."

Suspense clouded her already-cloudy features.

"No, it's from somewhere else. I've heard of you, but I can't say where."

"Well," I said, trying to get to the pewter duck she had brought, "perhaps you could tell me where you found this adorable creature."

"I know what it is! You're the missing Keyster! Yes. Barbara Walters interviewed you. It's you! The Vijay Blunder."

"Asunder. Vijay Asunder."

"It's him, everybody! The fifth Keyster!"

A crowd of older people gathered around. Because of their demographic, it took a while. Meanwhile, the great rolling lawns of a great English castle shone and sparkled. In the shimmering distance, its lions roared as faintly as a mouse. And all of England's heroes gasped in their graves.

"Be that as it may," I told her, "this is my life now. Could we go back to your duck?"

"It's not a duck. It's a merganser."

"Pardon me. A...would you get that thing away from me?"

Having been grafted onto a grapevine that this hyperthyroid American had started, I was fair game for every video camera that would be taken from the trunk of a car, a passenger's under-seat, or a backpack large enough to contain five apples, a Pomeranian, and a small bicycle.

"Please, don't do this," I implored these sound and image recorders, all of whom were staring at me through their cameras. I felt like they were sucking out my life force from the threads of my suit all the way down to the stemmyist of stem cells.

"It is him!" other people started saying as they jostled each other to be closer to me.

If the history of mob violence were examined for turning-points and fulcrums, it is when somebody says "It is him!" with the appropriate emphasis on the verb—which indicates a dawning of consciousness and a struggle with previous conceptions—followed by a wildly ecstatic intake of breath, then the cry itself. (The intake of breath is very important because it allows the person in question to project so much better than if there had been no intake and just an average gust, such as you and I utilize in ordinary conversation.)

My shriveling consciousness began to say "No, no, no!" as screaming hordes descended upon me with their cameras, old autograph pads (how do people come up with these things at such short notice?) and overexcited faces that were big in the eyes and mouth—like Miss Hyperthyroid America circa 2001. At such times, humanity is a great, grinning, gargoylesque organism that is as irrepressible as it is obnoxious.

"You're right," somebody else said, "It is him."

"Who?" asked somebody who was being pushed along and would have preferred to look at a Meissen figurine.

"I can't believe it! So this is what he's been doing all this time!"

"Man has to do something."

"A Keyster once, an antique dealer in his dotage..."

"Sad. Very sad."

"I was going to say that, but it seems so rude."

"Yes. It's all so very sad, isn't it?"

Rather than protest, I just let them surge. I looked at Miss America, with her enormous pop eyes and over-delighted smile and felt pity, though I don't know for whom. Certainly myself, who had been incognito all these years, slinking through my life, which I had to pretend was all right. But also, I think, for this undignified and almost depraved preoccupation with fame and celebrity. Here I was, an antiques appraiser living a perfectly normal life after11:47, and these people, through no fault of their own—a societal shortcoming, if you will—had come to expose me before the world, their fellows, and myself. It was then that I got the idea of shooting old Bruce, the only surviving Keyster, and also the only one who did not witness my humiliation in person. Yet, because he was the recipient of all the things I should have received, he had become, in the midst of this unfortunate brouhaha, which every goddamned cellphone and all other electronic devices known to man had recorded, my nemesis. His charm, his enduring popularity, as well as the initial affront, could not go unavenged. So, as all of these human gargoyles descended upon me with their cameras and their autograph books, I conceived of the plan for which I am now reviled the world over. I killed Bruce, the only surviving Keyster, link to a time when "the four lads" were Kings of the World. Every time a new song was released, it was shown on American television and broadcast to everyman and everywoman, who sat breathless as new sounds and words came into their dens and living rooms. It didn't matter whether they were Republican or Democrat; Labor or Tory—they all sat mesmerized in front of the telly and let themselves be stroked by the lads' latest contribution to civilized culture. The next day everybody would be singing it, with Bruce's characteristic trills, Jake's down-to-earth strummings, and Townsend's call-and-response. Marshall banged on the drums, but that was good enough for him. He could also smile again.

Amidst the dreadful clangor which had, for a moment, unseated all the rational impulses in my brain, I decided to take the high road and meet the crowd head-on.

"All right, then," I said. "Let's queue up, and I'll take you one at a time. Come on, you can do it. I know you can. I absolutely know it."

5

*T*he journey I'd taken to get to that moment, when my coldly vengeful scheme began to take shape, was a rather dull one. I didn't get into antiques right away. In fact, I got a job through Fitzwilliam Moultrie, whom I ran into on the street when I was wondering—now that I was no longer a Keyster—what to do with myself.

"Is that you?" he asked, mostly with his nostrils. His words were lavender-scented blasts of air and came at you from all different directions.

I turned around, grateful to be recognized. When I saw who it was, I was about to keep walking. I knew what he wanted. On the other hand, I thought I might be able to parlay his boyish attraction into something gainful. Though I haven't always been my greatest friend, I can sniff an opportunity from time to time and go with it.

"Hello, Mr. Moultrie."

"Now, let's not be so formal! Call me Fitz. Or Fitzy, to you."

He'd made a coup. I could tell it in his eyes, which sparkled with a controlled dementia. He was one of those people who had no outlet and walked around in an excited state, which would, in his case, be furtively, if temporarily, activated by people such as me. People who seemed to be on the inside of things, but weren't, on the strength of a second look, anything other than perennial outsiders.

I decided to go along with him into a tavern he liked. It was suitably dark—as befitting the nature of his desires—and it was "manned" (if that's the word) by epicene waiters and bartenders. Even the clean-staff swished a bit.

"Let's find us a little nook and beguile the time, shall we?"

He led me to a kind of covered booth, which reminded me of one of those canopy beds old people used to have. I always imagined these old people burrowing into them and getting lost until the alarm went off and dread reality dogged their heels again. It was on such a bed that old Scrooge was visited by his ghostly saviors. And from such a bed that he wafted through past and present. I've always liked that story. Small wonder. It's about timely redemption and second chances.

I saw that Moultrie was pleased with the even greater intimacy afforded by a little switch, which would lower the canopy, make little doors swing round, and force the kind of *tete-a-tetes* that lead to hasty exits and lurid satisfactions. If sex with a woman was a consummation devoutly to be wished, what might sex with a man—particularly when only one of the two parties might care to have it—be called?

"Now, I want you to tell me all about yourself," he said, moving as close to me as our table-barrier would permit.

Before I said anything, he pressed scented fingers to lips that blubbered together on contact. I watched the union of lower and upper lip and was transported to an aquarium where blobby creatures floated about in the murk. Their distinguishing characteristic was their resemblance to human squishiness—the bloated tissues people either suppress or, in my view, promote obscenely. Lip enhancement—mouth resuscitation, as it were—is almost as popular as the systematic augmentation of breasts that appear to challenge a seventy-year old woman's posture. I think it's why a lot of them go into yoga. It permits the kind of back support for which those who had conceived of breast augmentation back in the Dark Ages of Human Vanity hadn't thought of. You might say that when one segment of the anatomy is given a boost, what's left doesn't always catch up.

"I just want to say that I was absolutely mortified when I heard of your dismissal. I can say without exaggeration that you were the life-force of that group. The way you beat on that tambourine alone has ensured you a place in my undaunted imagination. And at the risk of seeming too bold, I felt that your singing voice was outrageously underused. I could tell that you were dying for the spotlight. Which—if those stupid gits did not eject you— you would have had all to yourself. I really mean it. When you sang, the others disappeared."

He leaned into me, looking this way and that. Why do people who are not being watched like to create the illusion that everyone is looking at them?

"I don't know if I should say this, but I've always talked you up to the boys. From the very beginning. I recognized your talent right off the bat. Oh, yes. You are special. Very special indeed!"

One of the epicene waiters came by.

"What'll it be, Oscar and Bosie?"

"Huh?" I asked.

"Never mind him. He has the satirical bent."

I observed Moultrie considering a swat with a napkin, but thinking against it. Yet having been recognized even in the way he had been, the waiter shimmied from the top down.

"Just saw a resemblance, that's all," he said.

"Well," said Moultrie, hardening his persona, "we're not paying you for historical parallelism, however accurate I would hope it to be."

With that admission, he laid his hand on top of mine. After a decent interval, I pressed mine as flat as I could and extricated it.

"Well, then. Tell me all about yourself."

In a matter of hours, I was over at his flat looking at etchings I didn't think anybody actually owned, but there they were: a roomful of Whistlers, Pennells, Muirhead Bones, Seymour Hadens and other people I don't remember. He'd gotten very friendly at that point and had slipped into something even more comfortable than the ever-loosening garments he had pulled off as we were taking things in.

"I won't disguise my attraction. That never does any good. I believe in putting all of my cards on the table."

He was sitting on a long sofa with rosewood accents. He patted the other side.

"Come sit down. I won't bite you," he said, with possible sincerity.

"I'd rather stand, if you don't mind. It's my preferred position."

"I suppose I could accommodate that," he said, twirling something that snaked from a pillow. The sofa was fairly plump with pillows and other accessories that were designed to cushion falls that would never happen in that place or any other like it. These pillows were fringed and caparisoned; cute little thinga-ma-bobs were pinned to special brocades. Neglected pillows seemed to say: "Love me and I'll love you back!" Some exuded scents that would roil one's stomach if it were upset.

There ensued a silence that could be measured chronologically, but I'd rather not think about it in that way. During that silence, "Fitzy" was sizing me up for what he might do with me on that day, and I was sizing him up for what he might do for me at a somewhat later time. I was just about to become interested in his part of the bargain when I heard a crash.

What the hell? was my first thought.

"Oh, it's Dragonweed. She's so tiresome!"

Very well. It was Dragonweed and she was tiresome. Reprieved by inward rumblings!

Then a knock.

"Can I come in, dearie?"

Moultrie put those fingers back against his lips, which he momentarily caressed, then said, in a stage whisper, "Mum's the word."

I didn't have to do anything other than what I'd been doing. I could strike a pose. Being onstage is good for that.

"Come on. I know you're in there. I saw a little boy who's grown up to be one of your circle."

I resented that, but obeyed Moultrie's directive.

"Besides, I really do have a problem I would like to discuss with you. I'll take just a few moments, after which you can return to your seduction."

Moultrie rolled his eyes at me. They denied the proposition while including me in. I didn't roll mine back. I didn't, in fact, know how to roll them the way he did. Gay men are underrated. They master so many trifling skills of which straights are not even aware.

"I suppose I'll have to let her in. She's done some really big favors for me in the past and, well, reciprocity is the way of the world."

Moultrie somehow found a standing position, from which he wobbled toward the door. For a man of his means, he had a very large flat. The room those etchings were in was bigger than my bedroom at home.

He came back bearing a largish woman—or a facsimile thereof—who reminded me of a featherbed that had been slept on by a person much like herself. She—or he—was softly round and dribbling all over. What flesh I could see was goosey, as if something had been plucked from it. He—or she —was clad in a nightdress with lace on the sleeves and collar, but was, for some reason, wearing jackboots underneath it—the kind that our friends the Nazis used to goosestep around in.

"Thank you for coming to my assistance. I don't know what I would have done. I really don't."

He—or she—avoided looking at me for some reason.

"All right, sit down and tell me all about it," said Moultrie. Who then said to me: "Would you get the lady a drink?"

"Oh, I don't want anything," he—or she—said, still averting his or her glance.

"Don't ignore the boy. Look at him!" insisted Moultrie.

The lady—or man—looked and let out a fibrous scream, which came out of a mouth so large that it seemed to emit thought-bubbles, such as you see in cartoons.

"Egad!" said he or she. "He's even better-looking than you said. I think, if he doesn't mutilate himself, that I will presently swoon."

He or she sank into the sofa, inverted a large palm, and placed it on his or her forehead.

"Oh, yes. I don't think I can take such a dynamic presence here. Perhaps, if he withdrew for a moment..."

Moultrie directed me into an adjacent room, which I had not seen before. By comparison, the etchings were coy little preludes to and obscenely uninviting tableau. I'd never seen male pornography before—and not much of the other sort either. Yet here it was, splayed out on couches, double-beds; in palatial interiors; prison environments—a sprightly gamut of place-possibilities came roaring out of tasteful, gold-leaf frames and archival matt-board. Of course, that was the least of it. Inside these places the goings-on were so candidly what they were that I found myself averting my eyes, just as that man/lady had done. I suddenly understood shameful curiosity. I will admit to wanting to see these goings-on because they were so absolutely arcane, but I couldn't bring myself to look. It seemed to me that, if I participated with my eyes, my entire sensibility would go along. Besides, I'd just had the humiliation of my life and I couldn't add homosexuality to it. Not, as they say now, that there's anything wrong with that. But then there was. In fact, it was bloody illegal. In essence, I was in the apartment of a law-breaker. By all the reasonable criteria of a fair-minded nation, he was an affront to the hard work and self-sacrifice that had gotten us out of that jam with Hitler, and was now muddling all of us through our greyish lives and shock-proof sensibilities.

I had never felt Absolute Paranoia before. Far from just possessing my mind, it suffused my entire body. It was as if I'd taken a drug that could completely possess its user. There was no part of me that wasn't involved. I felt it in my toenails, so to say; in the follicles of my luxuriant black hair, which is now completely gone, though I do wear a wig for it; along my upper thighs, inside of my stomach, grasping my inner ear. It was an everywhere sort of sensation and I was completely in its thrall.

"Are we amusing ourselves in there?" came Moultrie's voice.

"Yes," I managed to stammer. "It's quite educational."

"I was hoping you'd think that. I wouldn't want to do something you haven't witnessed secondhand."

"You're so naughty!" cried the man/lady, who was speaking confidentially.

I wouldn't hear anything else he or she ever said. In part because I intended to slink out of the room, find the front door, and escape. Which I did in short order. But, in the meanwhile, there was more...

There were no goodbyes, just a dratted look joined at the hip to an incredulous titter. Moultrie was melting down and the man/lady was having a little riot at his expense. I regret not asking this person what sex he or she had been saddled with at birth. I believe they call such people transgendered now. This person was a sort of rough draft, a coltish thing trying to stand on stilty legs. As I walked back to someplace, I don't remember where, I thought for a moment about how certain people live in this world.

Moultrie and this other person were, I considered, rather uncomfortable in it. As well they should have been. They were on the wrong side of the law—just as I would be so many years later, but more or less by choice. I'm of the opinion that such people are born the way they are and are obliged to make the best of it. All one can do is see the cards, pick 'em up, and play them according to one's best instincts—which some of us may come to believe are their worst.

Which is why it took me so long to establish myself in the antique business. No nookie, as they say—though I can't think of anything other than "cookie" to rhyme with it. And I'm not about to go there. Besides, I'm sure the gays have something better. In their way, they leave no stone unturned.

Nor should I say that Moultrie didn't get me a job. He pulled some strings and got me into a lorry. Having done that, however, he lost interest. He apparently had more grandiose plans for me. Or thought I belonged in a lorry and assumed I'd get comfortable there.

It took me ten years, in fact. Ten long years of lifting and hauling; ten years of driving through labyrinthine streets and byways only lorry-drivers and other genetic outliers seemed to know about. Ten long years of watching that twinkle come up in a fellow's eyes and trying, as best I could, to ignore it. I'm sorry, but I had to be my own man. I had to stake out life after the Keysters, though it was bloody difficult.

As I was making a turn one day, I heard their first international hit, *Crush Me Close, Sing Me Loud*, on the radio. I almost ran into an old lady walking her dog. Bringing up the rear was a younger lady who saw what I did and, when I came to a stop, banged on the lorry.

"You turned right into her! I mean, you didn't even look!"

"What's wrong with you?" asked another.

"A menace! He's an absolute menace!"

I just let them bang. I wasn't listening. There was Bruce singing the lead supported by those indelible harmonies—which I'd helped invent. While all of those people were ganging up on me, I wanted to spring out of the car and tell them that they wouldn't be so confident if they knew I was a Keyster. No, they'd grovel at my feet. "You know Bruce?" they'd all say. "Oh, what is that adorable Townsend like?" And: "Does Marshall ever say anything at all?" Then they'd start talking about Jake as if he were a combination of Lloyd George and Schopenhauer. Yes, a fresh new voice full of intellectual vigor. A mind that spins satirical gold out of a neglected schoolmarm; or lyrical pathos when two older people spy each other across a crowded room and can't, because of emotional scars that have plagued them throughout their darkly separate lives, get to each other. The Keysters were a wonderful conveyance that had found their place on the curbside of pop stardom—though they could scoot over and share it with a bit of High Culture when they wanted to. Was there nothing they couldn't do? And what a good song! Bruce and Jake were all over it: those two names that will ever be synonymous with The Inseparable Keysters. It made me sick—and thrilled —the first time. What can I say about having had almost fifty years of it?

Fifty years of the sort of idolatry that could have easily been mine. Fifty years of being polite to people I didn't want to talk to at all. Fifty years of hiding away and hoping, on the one hand, that I'd never be recognized again; and, on the other, to be sought out, not only for my association with the group, but for the indelible contribution I'd made to pop culture. On the first album was a song that Jake and I had written, though he commandeered it for himself. It was about the usual crap: lost love and the hope that never dies. It had a nice hook, though.

Don't you believe it, Oh no!
Love never dies, Oh, no!
It's lurking in her eyes, Oh, no!
Oh, love never dies!

I remember us writing that thing, not as a sudden inspiration, but as something you grind out over an unconscionable period of time and can't stand to think about when it's done. Jake was a hard man to work with. His grudging support of good ideas other than his own was, well, vintage Jake. When I came up with the first line, he refused to listen.

"How's that for a beginning?" I asked him.

"You live in a place for how many years? And you never see anything," he said, alluding to something he pretended to scrutinize.

I sang it again.

"No, you really don't. I think that would make one helluva tune. I mean, the idea of being in a place you hardly ever see, even during a lifetime of ups and downs, highways and byways. What about this for an opening?"

He sang something I don't remember, but I have a sneaking suspicion that he did and put it into a thing he and Bruce cranked out for a sweet little film called *It Was a Fine Day at Swinnerton's*. It had a bunch of unknown actors in it. Well, then they were. Now they're international celebrities whose laurels are paunchy enough to sleep on.

"I've got the first line. Why don't you listen?" I asked him.

"Huh? What did you say?"

"Do you not want to hear it? I know it isn't much, but it's a start, you know."

Said Jake like an old bobby: "I beg your pardon, sir. I'm hard of hearing when something big passes by. You know, like one of those double-deckers we've got. Just spangs the hearing right out of me. So I apologize for my inattentive ways. Perhaps you could run that by me again."

I started to do that very thing, but was stopped after a word or two.

"Oh, no. I've got to hold my ears again. Why can't a fellow catch a spot of quiet time? I mean, how did Wordsworth ever write his poetry?"

In spite of my irritation, I had to point out that Wordsworth had all of the Lake Country to himself. I had paid attention in my classes after all!

"Quite right," said Jake, still in character, "he did. He did at that. If you'll kindly wait a moment, I think I can be done now. No, let me rephrase that; I think it can be done with me. Yes, I think that's the way of it. I'm not causing this disturbance. It is, rather, causing the disruption itself. *It* is. And not me. What do you think about that? I mean, as a scientific proposition."

I waited until this quasi-disturbance evaporated and sang a few more lines, which I was able to invent while he was haranguing me. Those were the ones I heard on the radio—I mean, the first lines, the very first. There were more, and they were, for most part, Jake-ean inventions. And, for what it's worth, his were better. But mine got the thing out of the blocks, as it were, and I suppose I should be proud of it. Though I was not credited, there they were out in the open.

In his way, Jake acknowledged that I'd done something good. After he settled down, he began to invent his verses, while not relinquishing mine. Toward the end, when he'd made the thing stand up and walk about, he had me sing my stanza.

"You start it off and I'll come in afterwards."

So I did. With the lines I'd just heard on the radio. With the lines that would be my last. With the lines people would sing all over the world.

Unlike Jake, I didn't notice where we were; nor do I remember it now. I remember only one thing: the sound I made when I sang. I was in good voice that afternoon. And I sang my song, my stanza, with a warbling resonance that was missing in the studio recording that blared out over the radio and into the collective ear of England. It wasn't loud. The group would be loud in lots of places, particularly America, which it took by storm—due to Pouffy's shenanigans with the press—shortly after I'd heard that recording. No, it wasn't loud, but it had a purity that I've felt was peculiarly mine. It may have come from ignorance, an embryonic sense of what it meant to write something that everyone who catches a break knows inside of his own skin. Wherever it came from, it soared beyond the greyish perimeters of where we were and stopped both of us in our tracks. When I was done, Jake said, "Y'know, with a little Vaseline, you might go places, me boy. That's all you need, is a little greasing."

I have no idea why he said such a thing, but it wasn't a nice thing to say. Nor could I see it in the light of collegial fascination. If Jake meant anything by it—and how could he not?—I think he meant to say that, if he and the others had cared to work with me a little, there might've been a place for me. But I think his mind was already made up. Or so I would wish to see it. When you're a victim, you can make up any goddamned scenario you want.

I killed Bruce because he was the only one left. I also hated him, but I'd lived with hate for a long, long time and hadn't thought of doing anything about it until those people came at me from an old English lawn. It was as if the whole British Empire was telling me what a little thing I'd become through trifling choices, second-chance ideas, and fall-back positions. It was Peregrine I wanted, but he'd died in a suspicious manner that involved two male concubines, a peacock, and a brace of terriers. (The official cause of his death was a heart attack—very plausible, but not quite Pouffy's style.)

6

*M*aybe I'll say something about that now.

Strangely, Peregrine seemed to like me, in the early/early days, better than anybody else. When Sang Freud, our very first drummer, died of complications arising from the skin condition he hid more or less successfully behind his signature leather outfits, he transferred—after a suitable period of mourning—his affections to me. He was really after all of us, but Jake scared him, Townsend was a bit common, and nobody cared for Marshall until after the band became famous.

He was the one who'd recruited me from another band. It was my second part-time job, singing with that band. Once I lost the first, I found I couldn't bear to be off a stage, so I hooked myself up to the grapevine and joined an outfit that hadn't written any original tunes and, as it turned out, never would. Yet, it was smarmy enough to attract the slow-dancing crowd and *au courant* enough for the twisters—in other words, a plausible venue for the time and place. One of its members stayed in the music business, though in a small way. He opened a club—which happened to be the scene of a Major Moment in Keyster

45

lore: it was the last place the band played before leaving for America and staying there until it won the hearts of a nation that had not been similarly invaded for well over a hundred years. When they came back, they never played anywhere else again. They were too busy in the studio. Besides, Jake felt their concertizing had run its course. As had Bruce, who would always wonder whether the Keysters couldn't have drawn a hundred thousand people—as opposed to the fifty-odd that they were able to pull into Yankee Stadium. Jake said to some journalist that, if they'd showed up, unannounced, in Milwaukee, they could have done a TV spot and had every rutting teenager march on City Hall—or wherever that space needle thing was. When the journalist pointed out that the space needle was in another city, Jake said, "That calls for a tour, then. Call it "We'll Handle the Virgins" Tour and we'll split the proceeds with the anti-abortion group with the best costumes."

We were playing in this lousy club with no cover charge and some other house-band that thought it could get by with Elvis Presley imitations, and he, Peregrine, suddenly showed up. He always dressed like a businessman, in a bespoke suit, classy-looking bowler, and, sometimes, spats. Also: whenever he sat at a table, he liked to have a rose on it. Sometimes he brought a tall, narrow vase by himself, but as the Keysters got to be better known, it was supplied, sometimes with a visible, if not entirely adroit, sense of urgency.

So there he was for no apparent reason catching our set, which consisted of the usual crap: a few Peggy Lee songs, some Buddy Holly, and Delta blues, which I liked better than anything else. Eric Clapton told me, after I was interviewed on the BBC one of those times, that I'd made Mississippi a real place for him. "Just couldn't see it before you," he said. "And if I don't see something, I can't play it." I don't remember doing that, but it was nice of him to have singled me out. Of course, he didn't offer to pay me

anything for it. Nor should he have. I did what I did—
which was next to nothing—and he's a towering figure.
Another towering figure to make me feel smaller every day
of my life. (I've attempted to purge self-pity from this
memoir, but occasionally I think it should be retained. This
is, I will point out, winking, one of those occasions.)

Anyhow, there sat old Obit (that was his first name,
Obit) watching the band go through its paces and I
noticed, after a short time, that he was staring at me. Not
unlike Moultrie, he had his little signals. When I looked his
way, he sat up straight in his chair and primped. One time
he took the rose out and smelled it. But he *was* looking at
me, no doubt about it. Whether just at me is a moot point,
but I would challenge an Every Keyster Overview. By that
time, I think he would have been adequately discouraged
by the others. Or just not grooved to a radar that didn't
have a lot of mid-range to it.

When we broke for a bit, Haley, one of the band
members said: "You've got an admirer."

"Yeah?" I said back, pretending not to notice.

"That bloke over there. He's sweet on you. Better stand
tall, mate. One more week and we're outta this place."

Peregrine came up to me after the show and asked for
a word.

"What is it?" I asked with my signature combination of
willingness and hostility.

"I think I have an opportunity for you, though I'd
rather we talked somewhere else."

So we went to a neighboring establishment and had a
few words about my strong stage presence and infinite
possibilities.

"I just like to get with a bunch of blokes and make
some noise," I told him, truly enough. Like a lot of people
who miss out on things, I didn't think in terms of iconic
significance and world-class leadership until much later.

"Well, you make your noise more distinctively than
those others. I think I can put you in a better place, where

the right people are likely to notice you."

"All right, if that's what you want."

He was mildly offended. As I got to know him, he professed to have a business sense that was not in any way connected to personal interests. I suppose I believed him, but I cannot ultimately credit such mendacity. Of course, at the time, you had to be careful. There wasn't the sort of openness you see today. The love that dare not speak its name was whispered if it was spoken of at all. It was most definitely in the closet. I think, if it didn't have to be, Peregrine would be alive today. (No, he wouldn't because I would have gotten to him and left Bruce to his snowy leopards.) I never quite believed the story about the dogs chewing him to death. I think it was one of those fancy-boys he'd picked up. The peacock, however, worries me. I had no idea how that got in there. There had never been any peacocks in Peregrine's life. I knew. If there were any, I would have gotten wind of them.

I suppose you'll want me to say we became lovers, but that wasn't true. In fact, he used to get me girls in exchange for the privilege of watching us do what we did later on in the evening. Sometimes we just talked, which made him a little bitchy the following day.

He convinced me, as I was saying, to come to a Keyster rehearsal, which was held in a little shed behind Jake's house—or, rather, the house of his parents. The house had taken a bomb during the War, but had been reverse-gutted. It looked brand-new in places, and strangely bloated all around. I'd occasionally test a wall and it would bounce back, like a full stomach. What was in there? Kapok? Excelsior? Bodies left over from the Blitz? I used to wonder why some of the houses took one and a near-neighbor, standing just a meter away, was, by some trick of fate, immunized and didn't get a crack in its plaster. Said something to me about the arbitrary nature of catastrophe. It's where you're standing. When those bombs went off all over Iraq, I felt the same thing. The carnage was confined to a certain area beyond which one was free to go about his life. It was a kind of survivor's plat that was leading, for reasons unknown, a charmed existence. There was no charm among the rubble and the broken bodies. No, the charm elected to land a few meters to the north or south. Real people were leading the charmed life that had been vouchsafed those who'd been slower to get to the bad part or had stopped to check out something they'd forgotten about and thought that now was the time to get it. They'd been to market, slung a chicken underneath a spare arm, and tossed it in the pot. Tossed it there without thinking about anything but how tender the meat would be when everybody got home.

Jake's mum and dad, as well as his two sisters, were pretty obliging, when all's said and done. His mum even helped make us our first outfit, which I enjoy wearing to this day. In fact, whenever I think I've gained a little weight, I'll put mine on. If it's a little tight, I'll go on a vegetable diet and look good in it again.

My first look at the boys wasn't promising. Marshall was sitting by himself, woolgathering. Jake was listening to a Shirelles' song. It was one of a stack he'd put on the player, which released one at a time, like jukeboxes could do. Jake didn't just listen to a song, however; he changed it as it went along. And if a lyric was mawkish, he'd interpolate a corrective phrase, in the interest of retrospectively demolishing it.

"You ain't got a boyfriend, but maybe that's connected to your frigid ways," he said, with a bump and grind. Then he made up a full-blown response and supported it with a few wandering chords:

> *O frigid ways and strangled heart*
> *Give me, O give me, a better start!*
> *Let me settle under a gent who's well-hung*
> *And sing him a song his mum never sung!*

Jake looked at all of us expectantly. Would his revision fly? Or was it no better, in its own way, than the original it was meant to satirize?

Marshall replied with a drumroll. Townsend stroked a few perfectly symmetrical chords on his guitar—a fully-panoplied model encrusted with what would be called "bells and whistles" today. It was as unwieldy a thing as had ever graced a small man's body. Projecting from his caved-in sternum and absent pectorals, it looked twice its size. It was amazing to me, when I saw him hoist it, that he was strong enough to keep it aloft.

"Yes, I think that'll fly, boys," said Jake, cautiously vindicated. While he was clearly a front-runner, I got the impression that Jake would accept any victory—even of the shabbiest sort. Later on, however, he had no reason to think that he wouldn't prevail in almost anything—even after those cracks about the Catholic Church. He said the press had no sense of longevity—and he was right! In a week or two, it was on to something else. Only religious nutcases kept bringing it up.

Whereas Townsend was tall, but skinny, Jake had a wrestler's build—a wrestler who'd taken up smoking and slouched systematically. He seemed to be at war with his body, which wanted to stand upright even as he squashed it down. I'll bet some athletic coach had told him what promise he had had at something. Jake—who hated sports of any kind—would have taken the compliment and turned it on himself. *They're not making one of those iron-lunged idiots out of me!* And thus Jake came to impersonate an unkempt facsimile of a self that could never thrive, but couldn't be repressed either. Jake was the sort of young man who saw infinite possibility in himself, but didn't want coaches or teachers—or any other authority figure—choosing it. That comes through perfectly in a kind of personal anthem, *Beating On Me Bravely*, a mature look at a complicated personality, though it appeared early on and was consequently overlooked. Yet everybody's done a cover of it, so it would be hard to bemoan the song's life in the world.

Watch out, baby, I'll make you my slave
But don't get ideas because I'm on to you;
I won't get caught up in the things that you gave
Because I'm feeling my oats and I'm due
For greener pastures and a whore that's true-blue

Marshall was the least charismatic of the lot, but was as serenely self-confident as a chicken pecking about in a barnyard. On The Keysters' very first album, released in Germany and scrawled with what looked like Nazi graffiti, he plotted out a personal direction, which might be described as "among the guys, but not with them." Though the photographer had shot them as a group, Marshall had managed to find a private periphery and stay there. He was so self-contained that he looked almost pasted-in. But it was he who introduced himself first. "Glad to meet ya," he said to me in that offhanded sort of way everybody was affecting. But I felt that he *was* glad to meet me and was reassured. "You like me drum-set?" he asked me and let me bang on it. I could tell he didn't like the way I did it. I'd chosen the snare drum and landed a well-aimed stick to the very middle, which gave off a plunky sound. From the way I smacked it, no one would have singled me out as a drummer—or even the musical sort of person who didn't play an instrument, but had an affinity for the wildly distinctive sounds a flute and saxophone might produce. Still, I felt like a little boy who's been introduced to another little boy's inner sanctum. "Here. Sit on my horsey!"

Shortly after that, Marshall's humanity went into hiding or merely checked out for a while. Mostly, Marshall was absent. He seemed to like hanging back, even from the reputation a world-famous band might give him. He took it all in his stride, which was lean and loping. While

Townsend had a chicken neck and no chest, and Jake was at war with a body that might have distinguished itself in track or soccer, Marshall was perfectly comfortable with everything he had. If someone would have suggested the perverse reality of self-loathing, he would have checked the air, like some recently liberated animal, sniffed it—more out of a cautious curiosity than any eagerness to know it better—and gone right back into his hole. Marshall's sartorial preferences were not gaudy, but had the mark of conscious choices made over a lifetime of not knowing who he was or what he really liked. He finally settled on those dickie-collars that look so idiotic, from a fifty-year remove, in high-school yearbooks. On him, however, they looked plausible precisely because they were faintly ridiculous.

Townsend was making too much noise as he listened. Jake was what you'd call ADD today. He was easily distracted and couldn't abide competing signals, so whenever Townsend would say something like "That's a marvelous little bit, isn't it?" Jake would push him aside and tell him to shut up, sometimes with an epithet that was cruelly apposite. Jake had, by far, the most acid tongue and would, during the band's glittering heyday, be quoted in the newspapers all the time. He was the one who bragged about us being more popular than the Dali Lama. I didn't think that was so far-fetched. In fact, I didn't even know who the Dali Lama was. He could've been a Spanish painter for all I cared.

(He got into trouble, not with the Catholic Church, which kept its distance, but with its earthly acolytes, who would show up at a recording studio to lambast all of the Keysters for the godless renegades and false prophets that they were. One day, when Jake happened to be outside, he confronted one of them and nearly, as one might say, got into it. When the young believer—whose express purpose was to represent the Holy See—challenged him, Jake treated it as a lark at first. Then, without pausing to consider a more viable approach, he threw a punch at the guy, who decided he would become a martyr to The Cause and stuck his chin out. While sorely tempted to hit such an eminently available target a second time, Jake restrained himself and went back inside. The papers were full of pictures the next day, though the damage to the Keysters was easily contained. My favorite headline was: "No Two-Fisted Brawler, Keyster Smacks Only Once and Goes Inside", which was not so much a headline as a summary. Somewhere along the way, Jake had sold his soul to someone. No one but Jake—until the very end—could have been able to fetch so much goodwill with so little aplomb. It was as if everyone was rooting, where Jake was concerned, for the acceptable outcome that would leave him, and the Keyster "brand," unscathed.)

Freuddy wasn't there, but he'd drop in later on. It would be one of the last times he did.

"Boys, I want you to meet somebody," said Peregrine, who clutched my hand and held it out to them. Only Townsend came forward to shake it.

"Who's he? Someone you got off the bus to Scranton?"

"Where's Scranton?"

"I dunno, but would *you* like to go there?"

"It doesn't strike me as a tourist destination."

"No, and you know why? It's the second ring in hell. You take a bus there and you're on your own. It's like Brighton with more syphilis. Or an Industrial Revolution that hasn't been told to shut down. 'Hey, you blokes with the finger-burns, it's over. You can go home now!' Not in Scranton, you can't. They'll work you overtime as soon as look at you."

"Hello," I said.

They were apparently done with their hellos and settled back into what they were doing. Marshall had found a small rodent and was holding it up by the tail. Then he let it crawl around on his drumset. When he hit the bass, it scampered to freedom.

Peregrine stepped forward like a circus barker: "You gentlemen were complaining about your harmonies the other day. Well, I have a solution. I think you should try him out. A unique sound is nothing more or less than the melding of many voices."

"Yeah," said Jake, "well, we've got enough voices around here."

"Too many if you ask me," said Marshall.

"Just let him sing a little. Come on. Be sports."

"Well, it was you who found Marshy over there. And he can beat on that little drum, can't he?"

They all gave him a Bronx cheer.

"And you've been pretty good about hooking us up with financial opportunities. With all the quid we've got, we could probably hire us half a girl. Think half would do us?"

Another Bronx cheer, but not as enthuasiastic.

"Well, let's do it, then," suggested Townsend, more in sorrow than in anger.

"What'll it be, Caruso?" asked Jake.

"I dunno. Let's try 'Heartbreak Hotel.'"

"He's a brave one now, isn't he?"

"We don't want an Elvis impersonator!"

"Why not? That's all we are."

"Yeah, but I think we should keep the numbers down for a time when we'll all need to make our living that way. Fewer competitors, y'know?"

Banter filled the small room, which was junked up with Victrolas, sideboards, old crockery, and fucked-up heating coils. Old sheet music, of the june/moon/tune variety, was stacked on top of an upright piano. One showed a young woman in a schoolmarm's outfit: she was covered in fabric and so obscurely titillating that, when you studied her, you had no idea what you were excited about. Jake's handiwork, in the form of searing double-entendres, was all over it. Bathroomy scrawls—which suggested that all prim ladies were sluts at heart—completed his personal calligraphy. (As I would later learn, Jake had been to art school and gotten all the dirty bits in class.)

"How 'bout 'Love Me Tender' instead? If somebody's gonna piss all over something, I think it should be a ballad. I like to hear singers piss on ballads. Takes some of the sap out of them," said Jake.

"I think that's a splendid little idea!" said Jake, following up on himself and looking over to Townsend, who brightened up because that's what you did around Jake-O.

"Yes, I do," he said, "that's one helluva good idea," he said to me, imitating John Wayne. As you all know, he was a compulsive mimic. On the Dick Cavett Show, he acted out an entire Western. I'll have to admit that he was pretty good. I'll remember that bit about coveting sheep for sexual favors for the rest of my days. "In context," he said, "it was perfectly acceptable. Love the one you're with and all that."

The slouchy tempo that characterized their conversation was put aside when they put on their instruments: Jake with his Rickenbacker, Townsend with a nice little acoustic number, and Marshall with his booming bass drum. It was as if they'd breathed in these instruments, which assumed their rightful positions on chests and elbows. With his guitar in front of him, Jake wiggled in the Elvis manner and flipped on his tiny amp, which was covered in rattan and weighed no more than a small Chihuahua. When the band was going full-throttle, the amps were as big as refrigerators and had to be stevedored into every concert hall they played. Small wonder they gave up on public venues.

"Ready, boys?" he said, and we went into it.

After a moment's doubt, Peregrine couldn't have been more satisfied. As I crooned into a mike that failed, initially, to turn on, I fell into the thing as if it were a feather-bed and I a perfect sleeper. I could tell, as I half-sung and half-whispered, the words, that Jake and Company were mildly intrigued. Had they not been, I don't think Townsend would have called for us to do it again. I looked over to Jake, who'd been singing with me. He'd dropped the mocking tone and was mouthing the words as if they contained the most provocative messages man had ever written.

When we were done, we paused for a minute and looked at each other.

Jake said: "Not bad for a first try. Why don't we do an encore at the Fumed Oak tomorrow? Or is it The Dead Falcon?"

And that's how I got into the Keysters.

As Peregrine was driving me home, he couldn't stop telling me about how well I'd done, how much they all liked me, and that we were all going to get along.

"I can always tell. You really sold them. And these boys are a tough audience. I mean, once you get to know them, they're really sweet, but they'll put you through it. In spite of their apparent lassitude, they're very serious about music, especially the kind of stuff we've begun to call rock and roll. When I first heard it, I thought, well, this could be a field holler with some electric guitar. Jake said to me that I was absolutely correct. That's precisely what it was. But, like any musical form, it will develop, and I believe we are all on the ground floor. I feel so privileged sometimes. I feel like I'm watching history in the making."

He went on to tell me how his background was classical, but that, after he learned to play Chopin, he gave it up. He said there was nowhere else to go with it. He said he liked to play boogie-woogie by himself, but only as a hobby. His calling, as he saw it, was to get this new music, this exciting amalgam of blues and something else, out into the world.

"I've inherited money, so I won't have to work/work. Which means that I must succeed at promoting all of you. Nobody thinks I can do anything except play piano and manage table settings, but there's much more that drives me. Which brings me to my next point."

He put a free hand on my left thigh and left it there. Having practiced hand-removal, I set it back in his lap, which was showing some slight activity.

"Such a pity," he said. "I can do things those Casbah girls never dreamt of."

7

*B*y the time the Keysters really got going, I was still doing my lorry-driving, but I was moving up a bit. I had a girl, a flat, and some nice outfits. You might even consider me a kind of "man-about-town", though that mostly consisted of showing up places and looking fashionably bored.

It seemed, even then, that I couldn't turn around and not see the lads. Or overhear conversations in which Bruce or Jake did not figure prominently. What the hell happened to politics, I wondered? It was as if the Keyster Phenomenon had supplanted all informal communication.

A bloke I was working with when I needed some extra help wanted to talk about them. He thought he might try his hand at songwriting himself. Had a good ear, he said. Besides, how hard could it be? A central idea, and few rhymes, and you were home-free. (There you go. I've just done a little rhyme myself.) In spite of my better angels, his self-infatuation began to get under my skin. I'd not yet developed the easygoing detachment that was crucial, up until the moment I purchased the gun that would kill Bruce, to maintaining Life in the Present.

"Ever tried a ditty yourself?" this fellow asked me.

I rarely took on passengers, having come to the opinion that lorry-driving was an essentially philosophical profession, which made for a lot of alone-time. During the course of that year, my native pessimism became thoroughly ingrained. After 11:47, it had completely conquered that unknown territory that is neither mind nor heart. Some people call it one's "soul". Bruce—whose every thought was gathered by the press and sprawled out at one's breakfast table—scoffed at that idea. "Get yourself a nice scone," he said, "sharpen your pencil, and have at it."

Few artistic philosophies have been more succinctly expressed. Or more assiduously followed. When Bruce sat down and wrote his songs, which Jake would edit, he was as still as a predatory animal sighting a more helpless and supremely edible species. Pictures of him in his famous trance are more than unusually convincing. His dimples fall away, the please-you pucker of his lips subsides, and he becomes, through some sort of yogic transference, still as a shallow pond. Today, you'd call his focus "laser-like." And it was. Try to bother him and he'd not respond. He'd just sit there tuning into his private ether. That's how all of his most popular songs came out. When Jake was especially brutal with the blue pencil, he'd assume the same position, but for a vastly different purpose. When Bruce was mad at Jake he channeled curses—some of which were more ingenious, so word has it, than what got onto the page. A few curse words got into his songs, like the one he wrote about a Norwegian girl who had dumped him. After that, nobody could mention Norway in his presence. He even started to say "Fjord" as other people would say "Fuck!" But that was long after he and the others had dumped *me*. What I knew about them came from the popular press, or from profiles that appeared in fan magazines. When high-brow publications began to muse about them, the Keysters had moved so far away from pleasing the public that they didn't care to be esoteric either. They truly didn't give a damn.

"Before we address my struggles with the medium," I said to this prolific songwriter who thought that he could fall off a log and write a hit song, "what have you done?"

"Oh, this and that. You know, just me thoughts. None of them are really organized. But I'll get to it. I just need some inspiration."

I turned a corner which had been the scene of a recent accident. I'd presumably been an eyewitness and tried to re-create something I'd seen—when I was asked about it—out of the corner of my eye. It wasn't really fair. Mine was a passing glimpse, overlaid with so many others. On the strength of me having turned my head, somebody might have ended up in a docket. Or even thrown into gaol. It occurred to me that that was more analogous to song-writing than anything else.

"Inspiration, huh?"

"Yeah. It comes and it goes. Hate having to wait for it. It's like waiting for the next girl."

"Ever thought of looking at yourself in a mirror?"

The passenger side of the car was dirtier than the driver's side because of all the junk that sits in it when nobody else does. He reached underneath his bum to pick up something that had settled there.

"Whaddya know? A one-pound coin."

"There's your inspiration. Except that everything you find in this milieu belongs to me. You may stow it away in that little drawer in front of you."

He started to pout, this songwriter who needed inspiration to go on.

"I would beg to differ with you. This is my pound coin because you didn't claim it yourself."

"Tell you what: I'll stop over here and we can talk about it. However, if you don't put the coin in the place I have so thoughtfully and accurately described, I'm going to kick your bottom all the way to the River Liffey."

Like all cowards, he decided to get belligerent, then whiny, then belligerent again. After he'd run the gamut of emotions, he showed his true colors.

"I never catch a break. I find something, it's somebody else's. I get an idea and it fizzles out in me hands. I try to find meaning in the day-job and it eludes me. Why?"

Having known great gusts of self-pity, I wasn't entirely unsympathetic.

"Look, life is compromise. Life is waking up in the morning alone with the gas on and the people downstairs nattering at the tops of their voices. Life is staring at a mirror hoping against hope that the person across from you is not so green in the face and might be able to accomplish something other than pulling his drawers on and not shitting in them all day. That's life, my friend, and if you don't get used to it right now, it's going to start looking uglier than it ever has."

Amidst his tears, he seemed to be considering my views. In the meantime, I put the pound coin into the little drawer, which clicked shut.

I decided to level with him, not out of any sense of camaraderie, but because I wanted to steer the conversation in another direction. I've never had much patience for the chucked-out creator whose well has run dry and never figures out how to feed it again. He was one of these sorts and, while I had no feeling for him one way or another, I didn't want to hear him in this vein. Can't say it reminded me of myself; though, in a very fundamental sort of way, all failures are brothers. Some simply have more restraint or "class" or the sense of shame that tells you that nobody's going to pity you so you might as well keep your poker-face and smile out of it now and then.

"I'll tell you a little something about myself, but I don't want you blabbing it to anybody. Is that understood?"

"You haven't killed anybody, have you?" he asked, with the involuntary shudder actors are probably warned not to do on film.

Yet the irony of his question is, in retrospect, not lost on me. But it seemed rather comical at the time.

"One can do worse things—or have worse things done to them. Sometimes, the worst thing is getting through. Outliving a dream. Inhabiting one kind of consciousness, but living another."

During the course of that year, I contemplated suicide obsessively. And if I'd not been such a poor planner, I might've done it. London was very good for that sort of thing, with its gas-rings and snug little ovens. Strange about suicide: the people who succeed in doing it strike those not inclined as unnaturally resourceful; it seems that they could have put an equal amount of energy into finding purpose and meaning. But some people are more naturally disposed toward self-slaughter. Studies suggest that depressive personalities make the most reliable future-killers. They're so drenched in melancholy—so maddened by a sense of "Is this all there is?"—that they see no way out, in which case suicide strikes them as a reasonable alternative. On the one hand, they can't see two feet in front them; on the other, they have an overarching vision that would strike even the most suicide-averse as eminently sane.

"How d'ya mean?" the fellow asked.

"Let me give you a particular circumstance and I'll let you be the judge. Does this hypothetical character, that I will presently introduce, have any reason to live or does he not?"

At that point, I pulled over. I was at least twenty minutes early. It was a routine delivery. A little knick-knack that needed some polishing. I hated chandeliers. No matter how careful you were, you jostled something and it broke on the floor. Or you brushed against it as you were handling it oh-so-carefully and it chose, at that moment rather than another moment fifty years in the past, to cave in on you. No one had ever told me about the conundrum of chandeliers. To this day, I don't think anybody knows how to repair them.

"Who's this?" he asked, lighting up a cig.

"Open the window, please. Smoke makes me irritable."

"All right. I'll just hand-crank this little thing and out it goes."

"Thank you."

"You're not suicidal. Look how concerned you are about a little smoke. Bet you've never been to one of these hot clubs. Smoke in there, you can't cut it with a machete."

"I know of such places. When I go to one, I just breathe out a lot more than I do generally."

Thus I began a monologue in which I spoke of my association with a well-known singing group of which he would undoubtedly have heard; of my ignominious dismissal even at the cusp of fame; and, finally, of the lowly station to which I descended in its aftermath.

"I get all that," he said when I was done, "but what is this group? Is it someone I've heard of?"

Turning to the radio for the mental sustenance I needed, I started to hear one of a string of Keyster hits. A catchy tune, dashed off by Jake in a few minutes. (It had Jake's breezy cynicism, and was a harbinger of his screwy rhymes, which culminated in: *Feedlot In a Sinking Hole Hard by Newcastle.*) Some verses about going to bad places in a good car with a nice, firm-in-the-ass bird with you, then the bird's ingratitude.

> *You don't know, do you*
> *That I was getting through to you?*
> *No, no, no! You left me on the shelf*
> *Between old Hamburg and blue-tinted Delft*
> *In a motorcar without a motor*
> *And a glass without a soda.*

I listened to the song as if it were a much more complicated thing, something in the classical mode, with tricky polyphonies and gnarly arpeggios. I let the bloke watch me. If he had anything in his head, he'd put two and two together.

"You don't mean *them*, do you?"

I gave him that mysterious look you see so often in the cinema: the mystery-behind-the-enigma that has stoked, revived, and destroyed so many careers.

"You can't be serious," he said, with an incredulity I found insulting.

"What's so odd about it?"

"You're a lorry driver who makes 20p a delivery. That's all you are."

"Is that so?" I said to him between tension-tightened lips.

"I thought *I* was delusional! I mean, you think you could have been with them? I mean, these guys, they're at the very top of their profession. They were just in America on that really big show they've got over there and all the girls, I mean most people need just one—they could have thousands if they could make time for it. With us, time's not the problem. With them, well, they can have anything they want, but the irony is...the irony is, they can't make the time to get it. Isn't that ironic? I mean, isn't it?"

Suddenly I was pummeling the man: raining blows on face, arms, anything that wasn't protected. I felt instantly ecstatic as this helpless creature writhed and caterwauled, begging for the surcease that would not come.

"So you think they're out of my depth, do you?"

"No. Yes. I mean, maybe you were. You were, all right? You were!"

I wasn't willing to accept a coward's concession and kept beating on him. Whatever pacifists may say about violence, I say: don't knock it till you've tried it. Aside from those times at the Dead Falcon when we were, so to say, dead-on with a set, I'd never felt so absolutely triumphant.

"Please stop! I'm a very delicate person. I can't take any sort of violence. It's one of the reasons I can't work all the time. The strain of it, you know. My system closes down at the onset of tense feelings. Just feelings, mind you. Not this horrible, horrible assault. Please, stop hitting me. Like I said, I can see you among them. I just wasn't thinking the first time. I believe what you say. I believe it, okay? I believe it."

More in the interest of quieting an abject misery I was beginning to find distasteful, I stopped whacking away at him. When he realized that the drubbing was done, he ceased to put his arms up in front of him. Out of his bruised lips and punch-raddled face he squeaked another small concession.

"It's me, all right. I'm jealous of people. It's my nature. If I think somebody is thinking about something I might want, I can't help but want to make him suffer. I want to get at him, stop him somehow. I've always been this way. Guy at this clinic, he says I overcompensate. Seems to make sense."

Remorse is an interesting commodity. It always comes after some other, more satisfying emotion, like conquering a fear or putting it over on somebody. When all's said and done, we're not much removed from veldt and forest, when our animal nature espied the weakest member of a group and zeroed in on him. I've watched these nature shows that are "red in tooth and claw" and have had to turn away from them. My testosterone is flabby these days. Aside from the murder, I'd even call myself nurturing.

I felt somewhat badly about what I'd done—and in the name of my own vanity. I instructed the poor fellow, the slavering victim of my wrath, the overcompensating wormhole—to unclick the little drawer and take the pound coin for himself.

"Go on. You deserve it. If there were any justice, I should be clapped in gaol."

He reached in there, got the coin, and pocketed it. Once a coward, always a coward. He could have hesitated a bit, shown me the high road—even if he took the petty path to get there.

"What happened?" he asked me.

"To what?"

I wasn't thinking about 11:47 anymore, but the consequences of me starting to obsess over it. I know now that I should've gone into therapy, but these were tight-lipped days. You got hit, you picked yourself up, dusted yourself off, and applied for disability. Just joking—though our system at the time permitted it. Almost free healthcare. Now, when has another country done that?

"When they let you go...I mean, how did you react?" he asked, somewhat bravely, though he did raise an arm to protect himself.

"To tell you the truth, I didn't react. I was too stunned. I just couldn't believe it."

"Guess I would've done the same in your position."

Another Keyster song came on, the B side—which was every bit as good as the other. Jake was singing the lead part as Bruce and Townsend came in back of him. They'd gotten to be one smooth ensemble.

"Tell you the truth, I feel a bit aimless."

"Understandable," said my passenger-victim, who awakened to the sunny side of his passage: immunity. Once you get the crap beat out of you, you're not likely to have it done again. Besides, we'd found a sympathetic vein.

"We should do our delivery," I said.

"Oh, yes, we should."

"Just around the corner."

"Yes, it is."

"Shall you go on or shall I?"

I told him I'd go in. He'd done enough work for that day. I'd go in, get the thing, and make my 20p. And, after I was out of sight, he could make a run for it.

Which he did. If I were in his position, I think I would have too. Yes, I most definitely would have.

8

By the time the tenth anniversary of 11:47 approached, I'd relaxed my position about the lads, who had broken up a year before that and were doing projects of their own. I'd moved up in the world, looked prosperous, and had fewer nightmares about cascading down long flights of stairs into vats of boiling water (it was never anything else but water), being pushed from airplanes or allowed to sink into the quicksand a fellow explorer, complete with khaki shorts and pith helmet, had managed to step over. Gone also was the self-recrimination that always goes with a colossal failure, whether you're the cause of it or not. I shouldn't say it was gone; I'd just learned to bite into it, like some animal snapping at something it needs to kill.

Yet one evening, when I heard that Peregrine was giving a talk about the group's meteoric rise and regrettable downfall, I was drawn to the lecture hall, which, because the Keysters would never set foot in a recording studio again and had, after their long hour was spent, become a *legendary presence* and *mythic force*.

There were the usual groupies and busybodies; the academics and the talking-heads; the washed-up glitterati and the ostentatious bosoms that could be maintained, with the right budget, against good taste and reasonable expectations. I'd bought a ticket in advance and presented it at the booth. The guy there looked at it, then looked at me, and said: "Go on in. When you're there, you can ask about seating."

I was led to the nosebleed section by the kind of guy who ushers for a living—one of those people who live on the cheap but manage to see and hear everything.

"Aren't you excited?" he asked me, as we ascended into the Milky Way of the old theatre.

"Moderately," I said.

"You musn't be a fan, then."

"Not really," I told him in a "mind your own business" sort of way—which such people never seem to get.

"Too bad. Bet a lot of diehard Keyster-lovers would give their eyeteeth to be where you are."

"I'm sorry to pre-empt the faithful," I said, quashing further conversation. As he went away, he gave a fellow geek the cuckoo sign, implicating me as the crazy bird one gets now and again.

I heard people talking. They were as excited, in their overdressed, pawned-jewelry sort of way, as the wannabe insider who had seated me next to them. I looked at my ticket and saw Peregrine's full name: Obit Peregrine. I didn't think of killing him right then, but his first name must've planted the image of the old fellow lying etherized on a table. I could see him there, in that cold room, with forensics people fussing over him, but trying, at the same time, to be professional.

But the program was soon in progress, introduced by one of England's most sophisticated fatheads, Basil Gamaliel Winwip (pr. "Winnip.") He and I would talk at a similar program twenty years down the road. His toupee looked a whole lot better from leagues distant. A drunken lady might even mistake it for real hair. But his seething good nature and emerging pot belly were negative quantities even then. I wondered what he liked most in bed and imagined a longsuffering wife considering a request with a combination of lapsed affection and absolute horror. He was one of those repulsive people you couldn't feel sorry for, but couldn't blame either. They were what they were and they would always be that and nothing else.

"Ladies and gentlemen," he said, shielding his eyes from the beam of light that isolated him from all creation, "it is my special privilege to introduce to you a man who needs absolutely no introduction. He started out as a self-described 'egghead', but found, in his search for new styles and forms, four lads whose music is, even as I speak, being heard round the world. What could be said about our former glory can also be said about the Keysters. The sun cannot and will not set on the majesty of their music. Here, then, is the man who marshaled them to where they needed to go—into our minds, hearts, and imaginations. I think it is safe to say that the world is a much different, and indubitably better, place with them in our sights—and on our turntables. Please welcome the greatest promoter/manager of our age, Obit Peregrine!"

As the spotlight shifted, the crowd went up, as if sucked by an invisible fan, onto its feet. Applause such as Roman gladiators must've heard before the lions set upon them shook the old theatre, a remnant from Edwardian times and, of course, a reminder of The Empire's former ascendancy. All the great actors had played there, from Forbes-Robertson to Barrymore to Olivier. It was here, in fact, that the critic, Gosford Beach, had perished as Olivier, in an early incarnation of King Lear, decried the violence of the heavens while attempting to find a bit of sanity inside himself.

Then Obit came into the spotlight, crowding out our beloved emcee.

"I'm not much for words, my friends. But I am profoundly grateful that all of you could come here for our little chitchat. In that no conversation can possibly measure up to the experiences it describes, I have taken the liberty to bring a few pictures along with me, some moving at so many frames per second—I forget how many, please forgive me—and others that are divinely and enigmatically frozen. I hope such documentation will flesh out our *tete-a-tete*. Thank you. I will never forget this day—no, not as long as I live!"

If one thunder-roll could out-crack another, this one, for Peregrine, did. Not only was the assembled multitude on its feet again, but its almost-frightening electricity reached down onto the stage and swept Peregrine into its embrace. He seemed tall, grand, and not a little powerful. In spite of my feelings for him, I was almost proud. We'd had a history together that was regrettably short-lived. And yet I had crossed his path and he mine. History had moved beyond me, but he could—if he cared to—recall it every step of the way. As the lights shimmered and handclaps beat against the vaulted ceiling, with its irrelevant chandelier, I fell into as deep a depression as I have ever known. As we all sat down, the woman next to me said: "You know, this is something I'll tell my grandchildren about." I looked at this stretchy-skinned old cow and said: "You'd better hurry up with it. You're bloody well there already."

I don't think she heard me. A pity. Grand illusions—as Bruce said in the song—should be confronted head-on.

Such events are always vaguely disappointing, but that's not what I want to talk about. What I want to talk about is the "enigmatically" frozen image Peregrine trotted out, with the help of a projectionist, after he and old Basil Wannawip (as the irreverent among us call him) were about fifteen minutes into the interview. The insufferable old poofter was talking about how he strung the four lads together. ("And not from whole cloth by any means!" he said.) Very witty, I thought. Very witty indeed!

Then it was the early gigs, with pictures of the lads

playing at some of the hellish venues that seem to crop up when you need them. Then the Dead Falcon—or "DF", as it's known to insiders. Then there was a pause, during which I knew Peregrine—whose conversation was haulting to a fault—wanted to say something he was apparently struggling against. And I knew, sitting way up in the theatre's topmost tower, its aerie, its empyrean, that he wanted to say something about me. He'd just shown a picture of the The Bunker—as it is known in pop culture circles—which was the old shed in back of Jake's parents' house, with its manageable clutter amidst which the instruments of our trade were strewn. There was Jake's little amp, dead Freuddy's drumset—though Marshall had put the big bass drum in by that time—and Townsend's beautiful folk guitar, which, when they toured New York City, was signed by Pete Seeger, who regretted he wasn't Woody Guthrie—though that could be said about almost everyone, couldn't it? My tambourine was there too, next to the harmonica Bruce inherited from Jake and liked to trot out as often as he could. He wasn't very good at it, but he knew how to add piquant accents to a song. (Who could forget those keening high-notes he put into "No Love To Hide Because It's Gone"?) It didn't hurt that our producer, Sir Robert Villiers (he's a Sir now and why wouldn't he be?) knew how to posh everything together. The lads hardly ever credited him—no, not even for the string sections and harpsichord solos.

Anyhow, Peregrine had talked about Sang Freud, who was with the band for only a short period of time and made virtually no musical impression, so it should follow that he'd want to say something—if only in passing— about me. Such an omission might be called significant, if not irreducibly profound. Sitting there, I became intolerably restless. I tried slipping my hands, which had broken into a sort of independent sweat, underneath my thighs, where they twitched and drummed. Then I started breathing, as people who are meditating do: concentrating on the breaths as a way to un-signal distraction. I took one in, breathed it out; another in, breathed it out; and so forth and so on. But I could not quiet the rapid beating of my heart, which seemed to have leapt from my chest and into the crowded riot of my brain. Though I was not aware of it, I was muttering something. "Say it, goddamnit! Just say it!" But another picture came up—of the Inseparables touring—and my moment in the sun had vanished. The train had left the station, the wagon had pulled away, and no reviving gust might restore the permanently sullen moment I would live with in the decades to come.

"Shhhh!" said the lady next to me.

"What's that?" I said.

"Shhhh." She said again, without the exclamation. She didn't want to make a spectacle of herself. She just wanted to hear the people onstage.

"You want me to shut up, do you?" I asked her, as you'd say to a butcher who'd given you a bad batch of kidneys.

She nodded, with the dawning horror of someone who feels and knows she has set something off.

"But I don't choose to shut up, you see. I choose to express myself, just as those lads were doing before you, you, and you knew about them. What about it, old Peregrine? Where am I in your story? Don't you remember taking me away from that club and introducing us? Finding us those nifty outfits? Telling us we should grow our hair? I was there at The Creation, as it were, but you're just allowing for the birds and the beasts. What about the trees in which they might live? What about the streams from which they can quench their thirst? And the goddamned people who came after them?"

I was approached by the guy who'd seated me.

"Is there something wrong, sir?"

At that point I rose from my chair. Having been trapped underneath me, my hands flailed out. The one nearest him strayed and smacked his cheek. He didn't seem to notice it. Rather say, he noticed it as something that was likely to occur when he was in the presence of somebody like me.

"Is there something wrong?" I asked him back. "Is that what you're asking me? No, there's not anything wrong at all. No, the world didn't end for me at 11:47 on that special night when the lads, at that man's behest, convened in a smelly little room at the DF, as you call it, and said to me: 'This was your destiny, but it's not anymore. It's not now and it never will be. Goodbye, destiny. And fuck you, Vijay Asunder!"

With the mention of my name, some people turned toward me. "Who's that?" somebody asked. "Sounds familiar though, doesn't it?" "Now that I think of it, it does."

In the grips of my own Learish passion, I didn't notice that my pacificator was communicating by walkie-talkie. Before I got to the meat of it, men in security uniforms approached me and said I should come quietly.

"What if I don't want to?"

"None of that, sir. You need to come with us, that's all."

"I think we have a philosophical difference here. I want to stay, but you gents in your Buck Rogers outfits appear to be opposed to it."

One of them held out his hand, as if to escort me into a ballroom.

"Come along, then. We'll get you out and we'll have a little conversation."

"But I want to listen to this one. I am, after all, a part of it—though, when it came time to mention my name, it was suppressed. Little pussy-lips down there decided not to mention that he'd personally evicted me from the band."

I'm sorry to say that I ran past these uniformed cretins and bellowed out my rage and pain towards the two men who were way down below me.

"You could've mentioned me, but you didn't. Why? I'm as much a part of history as you are. I just exited the stage before the rest of them. And at your behest! Yes, you killed me, you little poofter. You killed me just as sure as putting a gun to my head or pushing me off the Eiffel Tower. I'm dead, you understand, and my death is your doing."

As I was dragged away, I heard Peregrine say to the other guy: "Delusion is a most pernicious disease. I hope they understand that and go easy with him. I really do."

Then: "That's remarkably generous, sir. It shows the fine, self-effacing character one rarely finds in a business like yours. It really does."

As I left the building, I could hear thunderous applause. I had never felt like such a negative quantity—no, not since that red-letter day that will live, for me, in infamy. Yes, I know that sounds melodramatic. Having been ejected from a rock and roll group isn't Pearl Harbor. On the other hand, it most certainly was. If it wasn't my own Pearl Harbor, it was nothing at all.

9

I think Peregrine was in love with me from the start. It seems clear to me now, but then I was trying to ride a little wave which crested at some two hundred feet and kept going and going. I wasn't thinking about much except honing my skills and trying to create a position for myself in the band. When we were at one of the lesser clubs, we had some rowdies in the audience who wanted us to play covers only. (We'd be introducing Jake's songs—as well as a few by me—and get shouted down.) Sometimes Jake would come to the microphone and, tapping into his Oxonion brain, attempt to reason with these people. We all stood aside for the lecture, hoping that he would come up with some syllogism, some piece of ironclad reasoning, that would silence them. But they started to throw things instead.

Gentlemen," he said to a bunch of Irish hoodlums with leather jackets not unlike ours. (Peregrine hadn't come up with our "Edwardian" look yet. Our hair was combed in the bouffant style, like a bunch of greasers from Hoboken.) "Human progress hinges upon new material.

Without it, we'd be stuck in Roman times. You know, going to public baths and smearing lead on our faces. Why are we in the superior position we're in now? Because, over the millennia, people have introduced new material. Mozart didn't just happen, gentlemen."

Because they weren't used to civilized defiance of any sort, they listened. When Jake made a point that interested them, they cocked their heads like dogs and thought it over.

"No, he did not indeed! Mozart didn't start off being Mozart. When he was going around with his piano, you couldn't say 'Lookee here, boys. Mozart is playing. *The* bloody Mozart!' And have a bloody riot on your hands. No, you could not. Mozart wasn't Mozart yet. But, thanks to new material, he would be."

"Wait a minute," one of the hoodlums said. "He had to be Mozart. Who else could he have been?"

His mates clapped him on the shoulder. He'd thrown a dart into the center of the target.

Jake rolled his eyes at us as we stood in a sort of parade rest. It was hot underneath those lights. The makeup we were wearing at the time started to run and irritate the eyeballs, which strained against the glare. But Jake was making the world better for democracy—a strategy I thought counterproductive. I wanted to turn up all the amps and blast them out of their chairs. Management generally frowned on that because it wanted to put bottoms into those chairs, no matter what kind of jejune mentality might be attached to them. At least Jake had 'em listening. They didn't always behave like that.

"He was Mozart by name, but not reputation. That would take years and years of showing up at venues not unlike this one, sitting at his man-sized piano, and playing his dear little heart out. Isn't that right, boys?"

We gave assent by voice, body language, lassitude. I suppose we could've been more enthusiastic. I did mention getting hot. And the makeup. And there were also our breeches, which were as tight as pantyhose. When we were just standing around, the waterworks unleashed by all the hot lights found every crack and seam in our bodies. I'd wiggle a bit; then somebody else would start doing it. Marshall got up and shook himself off. Like a dog. As you know, it became a sort of trademark in the movies they made. In every one, the screenwriter and director would contrive a situation in which Marshall would rise to his feet, give everybody that canine look of his, and shake something off. In the best bit, he shook off a mud-bath he was taking. When he was done, his pudgy little body poked through, with a fine mess of leg hair and undeveloped genitalia. His were the only movie genitalia that were never censored. I don't think Marshall ever got over that.

"So, gentlemen, I want to beg your indulgence here. I want you to think of us as bearers of civilized intelligence. I want you to think of us as pulling consciousness forward. Can you think of us doing that?"

They conferred with each other and let their spokesmen bear the message.

"What if you do this? You play one of yours and then we get to make a suggestion. Then you play one of yours and so on. How's that sit with all of you?"

Having won access to civilization, Jake was fairly overjoyed. The rest of us just wanted to get on with it. I didn't mind playing the old songs. It was all practice to me.

"Gentlemen, this is a moment none of us are likely to forget—a kind of bridge from one era to another. You have voted, all of you, for the kind of progress that made Mozart a household name. Whether it will do that for us, I cannot tell. But you have created a magnificent opportunity for us all—all of you out there and for us band members as well. You have raised the bar and made untrammeled creation possible. We will never forget this moment, will we, boys?"

We all said, with a trying sincerity, that we never would. But what did we do? We played a lot of the old tripe that had been original at one point, but was seen, even in that day, as warmed-over. Jake managed to sneak in a few of our songs, but I found his choices to be surprisingly conservative. It was as if, by winning an argument, he could promptly let it go. Perhaps it was the argument itself that was important. Jake liked to be challenged. These hoodlums had given him a splendid opportunity and he took it up like the shillelagh-swinging intellect for which nobody—having never seen one before—had name or precedent. Yet having satisfied himself with regard to these hoodlums' fickle sensibilities, he went on and gave them pretty much what they would have asked for if he'd not demurred at their choices. In this—as in so many other things—Jake was singularly perverse. He had to aim for something no one else wanted or had even thought about. When Bruce got into the band, Jake moderated this tendency, though it hardly disappeared. Jake needed someone or something to rebel against. Because Bruce and Jake were peas in a pod, Jake couldn't slash at the sheathing. At least not with something that caused blood to boil, leak, or become visible on an article of clothing.

When we were done, Peregrine met with all of us backstage.

"Nice little stunt, Mr. Churchill," he said to Jake.

"Oh, y'mean me little symposium? Yeah. I just get sick of those old songs. Or most of 'em anyway. If I never sing 'Sweet Georgia Brown' for the rest of me life, I'll be a happy man."

"I'll sing it," I suggested.

Peregrine thought that an excellent idea. The others weren't beside themselves with joy, but let me have the assignment.

"Yeah," said Jake. "I think that falsetto thing you do would fit right in."

"Whaddya mean, falsetto?" I asked him.

Somebody imitated me saying that, but I couldn't tell

80

who it was. It's what happens when you're the odd man out.

"Now let's behave," said Peregrine, ever the peacemaker, though I know our wrangling excited him. Whenever we had it out, he sat there in a kind of mesmeric condition, trying to remember it for future reference.

"The falsetto hasn't been exploited in rock and roll yet. Best not to reject any form or style until you've tried it."

With that observation, Peregrine looked over to me, eyebrows squashed together. I noticed that his feet were moving like Dorothy's in *The Wizard of Oz*. They were tapping out a wish he'd had, not for Kansas, but for me, I suppose. Below he looked girlish; from the neck up, however, he looked for all the world like an Arabian huckster. The eyes were inquiring: "Did I articulate that to your satisfaction?"

"I don't care one way or another," said Jake. "Just as long as I don't have to sing the bloody thing."

Like all leaders, Jake knew how to put you down. When he was done with something he didn't like, you found yourself not liking it either.

"It's settled, then. Vijay gets the vocals on 'Sweet Georgia Brown'. Perhaps we should rehearse it with him."

"Give it a rest!" said Townsend, who wanted to pack it in. Marshall was lackadaisical, but Townsend, with his long neck and easy fingers, wouldn't have done a lick of rehearsal unless he was strong-armed. Jake could apply some of that muscle himself, though he, Townsend, preferred to take direction from a neutral party. Peregrine was the right bloke for that. Nobody ever resented him making suggestions, in part because he was almost always right. He could inhabit the future and come up with the adjustments we could make in order to meet it head-on.

When we were about to go our separate ways, Peregrine slipped in behind me and said we should go somewhere, just the two of us. I was hungry enough for sure.

"Where to?" I asked.

He was momentarily at a loss for words, though I can't think why. He not only knew all of the fashionable restaurants, but the dirtiest dives in creation—which he very possibly liked better than the gilded cages that were the fashion of that day.

"I'll get my jacket and you can be thinking of somewhere," I told him.

When I re-joined him at the stage door, he'd recovered his composure. He'd lit a cig, which he'd stuffed into a holder. He didn't like to contaminate his fingers with that awful smell. He also worried about it infesting his clothes. He was a kind of visionary in that way: forty years before smoke-free restaurants became *de rigueur*, he was advocating for them. I grew sick of hearing him talk about his phobias. I just wanted to sit somewhere and fill my belly.

His car took us to an Indian place somewhere down in Eastcheap.

"Will this suit you, petal?" he asked, as we entered a kind of kitschy temple. The sitar Townsend would eventually use way too much on those otherwise ground-breaking albums, particularly *St. Wherewithal's Saturday*, was twanging, incense hung implacably in the air, and small, brown-skinned people were running about with hot plates in their hands. It would be unkind to say that the usual gibberish was circulating from waiter to kitchen staff to worried *maître 'd*. I'm sure our Mother Tongue holds little charm for people who have so often had to hear it from the overlord *du jour* or colonial in-betweener. My name is Indian, of course, but it comes from neutral territory. I have no recollection of "Memsahibs" and all the rest of it. When I was born, India was straining toward independence and would get it soon enough. Even so, my background has been connected with the murderous rampage that now defines me. Some have asked, with a touching naiveté, why somebody from a formerly oppressed nation—which earned its freedom by turning the other cheek—would want to do something so heinous? I can't think of a sillier question. When has one's forbears silenced unspeakable impulses, let alone the occasional unkind word?

"Yeah, this is great," I said, sitting down with Peregrine in a booth that wasn't as intimate as the ones we generally shared, but was pleasantly cut off from the brouhaha of waiting and serving. When the kitchen door swung open, I was reminded, in a somewhat brutal fashion, of where we were. We could have otherwise been in Rangoon or some other exotic locale.

"I'm so excited for you!" said Peregrine, who, suiting action to word, tipped over the water glass he always ordered for himself. "Dry mouth," he always told me, with a subtle, but unmistakable, lubricity.

"Oh, you mean about the..."

"Exactly! I've wanted you to be able to spread your wings. And now's your chance." Ignoring the puddle he'd made, he leaned over to me as men and women do when they want to exchange some delicious secret. "I think this is a turning point for you. And I'm so glad Jake and Townsend were so passive about it. I thought we'd get into a row."

That was rather odd. Jake generally gave little ground unless he knew he could take it back whenever he wanted. And perhaps he was thinking along these lines with that song, which he sang on one of the few really lousy records the band made. It didn't suit him at all. I sang it as well as it could be sung, but given our approach to music-making, it wasn't a good choice for us. You can hear it on the audition tapes that were released after Jake's demise. It just didn't do anything for him—or for the band. When I sang it, though, it was nearly successful. Even Marshall said I'd done something new with it. "Gives me something good to back up," he told me, out of earshot of all the rest.

I couldn't maintain my forward lean for very long. I

began to become conscious that old Pouffy intended for us to be dating, like boy and girl. I wanted to disavow it, but he'd done this *thing* for me, and me alone. I wondered, with a kind of boyish innocence, why he had singled me out. He was attracted to some of the others, but in a sort of general way—like any guy's attracted to a group of women who "show" very nicely when on the town or in a school picture. You generally find the one you want and ignore the others—at least for a time.

"Aren't we glad?" he asked, with that soon-to-be-crestfallen drop in the vocal register.

"Oh, yeah. I think I'll do all right with that song," I said, clutching it to myself. I was sure I could do it well enough, but, as with everything that's taken up without a thought, doubt started to gnaw away at me. What if, I was thinking, I couldn't do it? What if I was overreaching? What if my sudden status came from Pouffy's erotically tinged fixation and not any demonstrable talent on my part? When they get their proverbial chance, some people fail to shine. I could easily be one of them. Why not? Even in its infancy, rock and roll was already strewn with overreaching sorts who had strutted upon the stage in an attempt to unseat Elvis, only to be ushered, by the crowd's deadly nonchalance, into oblivion.

"Oh, you will. You absolutely will! It will showcase your most glittering attributes. Your smouldering romanticism. Your somewhat haughty, but engaging, sense of irony. Not to mention...no, not to mention your vocal range, which I must confess is so much steamier than the rest. Jake's got his confident airs and Towny's all right with backup. And Marshall, well, he does what he does, but you...you have undeniable power and presence. When you're doing something, I don't even look at anyone else. I just look at you."

With that confession, his long eyelashes went up and a couple of moony eyeballs confronted me. If this wasn't love, it was a moisty-eyed facsimile. I remember hearing

-called "Salzburg Footage"—shot by an amateur
r who would make his mark as an *auteur*—where
d every night for a month. If you don't think there
nistry between us, you don't know about fire and a
e. When we were really cooking, we burned the
wn. Nobody wanted to follow us because they'd
ak and gibber. Or seem to—which is the same
hing. Perception makes the world, no matter how
hted or shadowy it might be. If you think
ng is so, it is. It just is.

something similar from Moultrie, whom I hadn't seen for a while. It's as if the two had the same play-book. Or maybe all inverts thought in a similar way. Both Moultrie and Peregrine approached their erotic fixations as if they were breathless heroines. Their wistful attraction made me feel like some guy who'd just ridden up on his oversized horse—or, rather, steed—and was facing life with an indomitable restlessness. If nothing else, it made a fellow feel bigger than his boots. Or breeches. Or anything else these moony-eyed creatures wished you'd unbutton for them.

"Well," I said, trying not to stammer, "I'm indebted to your dedication to my career. I really am."

"Yes, but I could be dedicated to so much more." With that, he put his hand on mine, which, after a few clammy beats, I withdrew. "Do you understand what I'm saying?" he asked, moony eyeballs boring into me.

"Uh...can we have an appetizer?"

That put him off long enough for me to excuse myself. In the loo, I pondered the only possibility I had. And if the window had been larger, I think I would've climbed out of it. A Faustian bargain was being struck. If I didn't take it, I'd become, in all likelihood, fortune's bloody foot-soldier, with a bum leg and a sheet-sized bandage covering a head wound that would never heal. I considered what might happen if I went to bed with a poofter, and it terrified me. Every man entertains troubling suspicions about his sexuality. Sometimes he'll hear a fluty note in his voice, or watch a too-exuberant gesture fly away from his hand. Perhaps he'll be listening to some torch singer and start to follow the beat of it. Then he may even want to vamp.

As I exited the loo, however, there he was.

"I was worried about you, so I came here," said Peregrine, who was sweating. I'd never seen any moisture on him—at least not of the seeping variety. He seemed to be in perfect control of his bodily fluids. I was, however, convinced that I didn't want him fooling with mine.

"I'm fine," I said. "Couldn't be better."

"I'm so happy to hear it. I wouldn't want you in anything less than the peak of health. Look at you. You are an alarmingly attractive male specimen. Even here in this dungeon light. May I kiss you?'

Fortunately, one of those brown-skinned people whose hands must be genetically adapted to carrying hot things barged into us. He managed to keep the plates out of harm's way, but jostled Peregrine, who let out a parrot's shriek.

"What on earth are you doing?" he said to the man who had upset him.

The man attempted to gesticulate an answer. Imbibed in a commercial atmosphere, his English probably consisted of "Good evening to you, good sir," "It was a pleasure to serve you," and "Sit at *that* table, thank you very much." Meanwhile, he was juggling his plates, whose steaming dollops of *tandoori* chicken and overcooked chickpeas were adding more vapor to an already-steamy environment.

"Just go," said Peregrine, put out for the very first time since he'd recruited me from that other band. The waiter righted his balance and moved down the hallway, where he made a hard right turn into one of the restaurant's many serving areas.

"A moment has been ruined," Peregrine said, pouring a lifetime of near-misses and purplish regrets into a single phrase.

The rest of the evening was morosely uncomfortable, with Peregrine sighing out his frustration and me trying to invent conversational gambits that might get us through our dinner, which I attempted not to wolf down.

"You don't know how difficult it can be," he told me. "Having such feelings as I do. Sometimes they build up inside me and I feel as if I might strangle on them. I've even gone to a specialist, who said he might cure me. Well, so many hundreds—even thousands—of pounds later, I'm

stuck with all these inconve compulsions. I should have my persuasion, and I'm uncomfortable. I should neve my vision for rock and roll, from the very first barbaric astute and dedicated promoter

What could I say? He'd ju got to give him high marks for Until he turned on me. I supp eventually do, I would have fou sexuality, which was not the ki Queen to know about. Queen to

"Sure. You've done us a w make great suggestions and you' the time. I'm really grateful for you putting me on the stage with

"The Keysters! That's the na Keysters. Just came to me this think?"

I thought it was a terrible nar good instincts. I was smart enou really catchy. Which it was. Say "I sticks with you. Why that is I Peregrine knew. Perhaps he was them all. Perhaps that's why I car what he did to me. And why? Be affection that spoke its name just bloody closet. I learned somethin, that no one is above his desires and you have to minimize—or even d you alive. In my case, they cut a bigg person. They came, like so many ma eat me alive as well.

Everybody knows what he said a said I was a "test-tube burner." By wl chemistry didn't meld with the other

10

I had thirty years of near-comfort before I conceived of the plan that culminated in what the media has called "The Assassination of an Era". That's what it made of Bruce's demise. He was now An Era. God, the cheek of fame! Or, rather, its uncontrollable delusions.

It's funny, being here, in this godless/godawful place with my memories beating against everything that's being said about me. I must be one of the most hated men in history. To have offed a cultural icon, a Leading Spirit, and a world peace advocate—all in one fell swoop! *And* the sort of vegetarian who puts his money where his mouth his. Oh, yes. Bruce became such a passionate advocate of animal rights that he'd show up on the ice-floes and make films of seal-pups being bludgeoned to death. Yes, Bruce the Hero of All Mankind, succoring the weak, giving concerts for the needy, speaking Truth to Power. Out on the ice-floes with his camera, in the courtroom with his sing-songy voice, on the world's computer monitors with a perennial hit parade that will never stop as long as there's live—or, rather, dead—streaming. He let another pop star purchase rights to a number of Keyster songs. Why? I think he just liked to rub all of his stage-properties in everybody's face. However, one cannot deny that there were a lot of them: some four hundred songs written over a seven-year period. He was doing his own projects, but nobody cared about them. When he did a concert, the audience waited patiently through his work with The Viands, then Lot-With-Yard, and that other one I can never remember. But when he started in on The Keysters' stuff, the crowd rose to its feet, clapped, shouted, keened, wept, and generally went into a frenzy. When I snuffed him out, I not only snuffed out a single Icon, I snuffed the hopes of other life-forms, who—if they only knew it — depended on his promotional savvy and infamous good will.

I ran into him a few times and he was genial enough. Asked me what I was doing, how things were with me mum—who didn't live to see my infamy and wouldn't have talked to me about it if she had. I'm glad she was spared the hounding that would have accompanied her scant, and hardly showy, appearances in the public eye. She would have become one of those media-plagued relatives who, as "sources" would announce, resided in an undisclosed location. God! How brutal those prying bastards would have been! Some TV psychologist has advanced a suspicion that the seed of my murderous impulse was planted during those early years when boys are so susceptible and their minds aren't developed yet. I read an article in which some Ph.D suggested that, because my own father was killed prematurely, I needed to take a life myself. He called it "morbid patriarchal indentification," which was just another way of saying I wanted to avenge my father. Which is absolute bullshit. My father would never have endorsed that sort of thing. Nor do I. I killed Bruce in an almost monastically calculated mood for which explanations may abound, but will never come to grips with the temporary loss of reason that makes such an action possible. No, it is not a loss of reason. It is a willful suspension. It is a condition that exists between reason and that other thing that prompts us to do extraordinary things—whether they turn out to be "good for mankind" or not. Of course, I'm not going to plead anything like that. I may have been insane when I conceived and executed the act itself, but I was a cold-blooded chieftain in the planning of it.

For a moment, I want to get back to me mum and dad as a way of vindicating them. And also advancing my story, which should embrace one's friends and family.

They couldn't have been more ordinary. In fact, my dad was the most unimaginative fellow the world has ever known. Went to his little job with the railroad, got his paycheck, and lived as quietly as a human being possibly can. His greatest achievement was his unoffending nature, which made him disappear from a crowd and stay in the background of his own life.

Yet he had another side that I found chilling.

I once listened to them conversing in bed. Mum was asking him why he wouldn't touch her. He said to her that that sort of thing wasn't seemly once a child is born. "We, the parents," he said, "must dedicate ourselves to nurturance." Then she said that human beings didn't stop being human with the arrival of a bouncing baby.

"I'm not claiming that at all," he said. "We are perhaps more human as caretakers of another being."

"But what about us? We're human beings too."

There was a plaintive note in her voice—something I would hear rather often. But I would hear other notes too. I much preferred me mum miserable first and masterful second. Call me a chauvinist—or is there some other word for it now?

"We reach our highest fruition as human beings in sacrificing ourselves to others. Our humanity is never greater than when we deny our own desires in the pursuit of parenthood."

"If you don't touch me again, I don't know if I can bear it."

"You can, my dear. Just think of your son. Think of how much he needs you. Think of the person he'll become—the better person—if you dedicate your entire being, all the way down to your cells and tissues, to his development."

"Can't one do both?"

Here she took it down to a lower register. His voice was fluty, like Charlie Chaplin's. Hers could have colors and contrasts that occasionally touched me, though I didn't like it at the time and chose to think of the feelings she invoked as things best swept under the rug.

"No, I don't believe one can. I know I can't. When I think of you in that way, I feel like a rutting animal. I feel shame at my own brutal needs. When I think of our boy, however, I enter a new place. In a sense, I am reborn. All of the shackles of desire are sloughed off and I'm a more complete person in my pure sense of mission than I would have otherwise become."

"Can't you do it for me?"

"I would, my dear, but I find your selfishness off-putting."

"It's not selfishness. I want to be with you in the most profound of ways. Sex..."

"Don't use that word. Not in this house."

"...is sharing."

"I'm sorry, but I cannot believe in, endorse, or—needless to say—enact your premise."

I sometimes wish I hadn't overheard that conversation. It colored how I felt about them. More than that: it provided me with a knowing-too-much perspective that not only drowns a sneaking innocence like a warm puppy, it gives the bearer an omniscient sense that shouldn't happen until much later on. I'd see him reading his newspaper. Rather than going about her own business, me mum would look at him, first with a kind of tenderness, then with a dawning rage, and, finally, with a seething hatred that would come to disfigure her. Pictures of her as a young girl show the unclouded expression of the young. So little has been impressed upon it that it tells you nothing. As she aged, her mouth became tighter, with a pulling around its corners and a coarsely embittered expression that came to define and delineate her entire face. Before the conversation, she made her little dinners so quietly that you'd know them through the aromas that spread through our flat. After it, her preparations became audible, with pots and pans clanging together, portions of food dropped, and the boiling phases protracted. I went in there once and asked if I could help.

"You mind your own business," she snapped.

"It's just that I...you seem to be upset about something."

"I'm not upset. This is just the way I am now. "

I turned down the gas on the cabbage, whose rolling boil was spitting water off the sides of the pot, as if a storm were brewing inside it.

She turned it back up.

"I don't need your help. Now go and wash up. And tell your father. No, don't. He'll know it because he knows everything about how a household is run, who does what, and how well it is done."

Then she got up close—the very worst part for me, but necessary to her evening ritual.

"And how do *you* feel? Are you sufficiently nurtured today? "

"I dunno. I guess."

"That's good because we wouldn't want anybody not to feel anything less than completely satisfied."

"No. I suppose not."

The pot had boiled over. She contemplated it for a moment. I was about to turn off the flame but knew I shouldn't.

When she took the action she did, I'd like to say that I

was taken off guard, but I wasn't. Though I don't remember what I was thinking at the time, some part of me was probably bracing for Ground Zero. I'd been watching her too closely not to have an ominous sense of what she might, when pushed or under the influence of her beetling imagination, do. I saw it coming, first in her eyes and, finally, in the way she picked up the thing and aimed it at me. Yes, she *aimed* the thing at me. I could see it in slow motion: her finding the potholders, putting them on, yanking pot from stove, and then hurling it at me. I could see each and every step, as if it were a kind of family choreography that I might have to learn in order to retain whatever status I had achieved as an unloved child—or, rather, a child who had taken love from a spouse and not done anything useful with it. But I also saw her eyes, which bugged out over the steam that rose up when she grabbed the pot and threw it. The bugged eyes that stayed bugged through the emerging catastrophe she wanted, for that moment, to create. She wasn't after me necessarily; she just wanted to escalate the tension. How dare he sit and read the newspaper! He likes the radio on, but it's got to be quiet, like it was tiptoeing around him. Why should *he* be allowed that privilege? She wanted him to hear the crash, the water pouring out, the steam rising, and her off to the side, looking triumphant. Or mad. Or both. He'd know why. Oh, yes, he'd know why all right, but it wouldn't affect him. Nothing ever did. He was the Stoic Dad who had faced down Hitler's barrages and come to live an impeccably decent life, as if to atone for the world's evil in his own person.

Because he hated what he called any sort of "ruckus," Dad showed up as the cabbage started to steam in places no cabbage of ours had never been: on countertops, tinned goods, and the new tablecloth that would have been spread had this not happened.

"What on earth...?" was his question.

"Never you mind," she said to him. "Just a domestic

accident. Just me not finding the serving dish. Sometimes I do that, you know. "

Dad told me to go to my room.

"I didn't do anything," I said.

"I know you didn't. I just need to be here, alone, with your mum."

"Is she going to be all right?"

"Of course she is," he told me, with one of his beatific smiles. I noticed, for some reason, that she looked very pretty, as she was in some of the pictures we'd take down and look at.

I took my dinner that evening with him. By way of explanation, he told me that she wasn't feeling well. And ate somewhat hastily with a good appetite.

There were more incidents like that, which stopped abruptly when he died, or was murdered, or however one wishes to see it. At the time, I didn't quite understand it, which provided the insulation I needed to get along at school; keep my wits about me in between that and home; and wipe my arse with a sense of its loftier purpose, which was to be a Clean Young Man so I could get married and sit in front of a tubed television and, like my father before me, contemplate its mysteries. One day a schoolfellow asked me what was wrong. I guess I was moping around, not as kids do without trying, but with a sense of greater urgency. When something significant happens, people know it. A lot of 'em don't care. Some wish to exploit it for their own purposes. And some are merely curious, as this creature was.

"You all right?" said he toward my face, which was turned away from him. I never looked at anybody when I was young and fell back into the habit after the Keysters dumped me. If you looked at me, I seemed to think, you'd see nothing. I don't remember what I was thinking when that coal-scuttle of a Major Void crept over me. I was just a kid like many others.

"Sure. Why wouldn't I be?"

He shifted on his feet and threw a stone at something. There were always stones underfoot, just as there would be grass in Ireland and blowing newspapers in New York City, which I've visited now and again for an interview. Jake lived there for a time, but came back. When things got hairy later on, he was, because of his outspoken views, *persona non grata* there—not with the young, but with its bayonets and its bum-holes. Said he liked it—as if his opinion mattered more than mine. Which it most certainly did. I'd steal in there, stay in a moderately priced hotel, and walk around in a completely insufferable anonymity. I'd even pretend to be recognized and recoil, as if to make myself as small as I needed to be. My favorite thing to do was to duck, when fleeing an imaginary fan-base, into a small restaurant. There, amidst a pile of souvlaki or a steamtable that obscured the faces of born Irishmen, I'd hang out until the coast, as they say, was clear. Though it would always be clear for me. Always.

"You look like you've been thinking."

"Guess I have," I said. I'd never had many friends. Didn't think I cared to. It seemed as if everybody else had constructed a privet-hedge that interfered with, but also facilitated, the social processing that is so necessary at that stage of life. On one side of it, *they* moved about with the sloppy dedication that would, over time, become as smooth as silk. On my side...on my side, I could watch them doing what they did, but they could ignore me completely. And now this classmate of mine, in his steamed pants and tomato-colored cheekbones, was offering himself to me. Outsider to outsider. Or, rather, samaritan to chump.

"Yes, you look rather peaked, if you don't mind me saying it."

I couldn't decide and chose to be forbearing.

"We all have problems."

I assumed that he was right, though I'd never thought about it. I'd not defined my life as something good or bad.

Or, rather, the bad things were separated from the good and were therefore irrelevant. Perhaps what I needed *was* a problem. According to this fellow, one might have been there all along.

"Like what?"

He took another stone, but didn't throw it. He even shook it a little, so as to feel it inside his hand, captured there, and warmer than it had been since something had mauled it, softened its edges, and spit it out.

"Problems are not always large, but I've found that we think about them more than...more than any other thing. Personally, I find them interesting. So when I saw you, I felt that you must have one. Do you?"

To such a forthright question, I answered forthrightly: "My dad. Got killed. In an accident. Wasn't anybody's fault. Just happened."

"You're the...I heard that somebody's dad was killed on the road. Must be you then."

"It is me," I acknowledged. And, as if to set aside all doubt, I said: "Two months ago. A car hit him. Out by...yes, that's what happened."

He took the opportunity to hurl the stone, not at a neutral quantity, but at something that would have to mind it. Before it landed, a bunch of pigeons swooped away with that percussive sound they always make. They lived in a dangerous world and were always bracing for its consequences. When something came at them, they were already on their way. One time I came across one that was slightly injured, but hopping around like an athlete who wants to get back into the game. His unseemly fragility was in stark and stony contrast to a small Catholic church, cobbled into place during the previous century with "Hail Mary's" and hammer-blows that had found, as our Heavenly Father had, a place to land and dwell for as long as people were frightened and despairing enough to show up. It was the sort of place that didn't feel right unless you slapped against it. A place not to be stepped-over or gotten around. A bombed-out twin brother stood next to it, as if to show what might happen to the non-believing. Though I saw no words, it might have been inscribed with the slogan: "Abandon hope, all who enter here." People were walking about, but, when they saw me, they scattered. If someone (or something) got stuck here, well, it was just too bloody bad. I looked around, as if to establish where the pigeon might've come from. I thought a mother-bird might come down and take it away, but I suddenly knew that if I wanted it, it was mine. What power to have over a helpless creature! After it settled into my hand, emitting miniature bird-sounds, I wanted to get rid of it. What was this frail and frowsy thing to me? But how? If I pitched it up into the air, would it fly away or plunge to the cobbles with a sickening thump? Weren't all creatures endowed with the will to survive? Or did they have to grow, as we did, into their little bodies first? If they didn't know what they were protecting, why bother? "Come on," I said, "fly now. Fly away and find yer mum." But even then I knew that if I didn't take care of him, the creature was doomed. "It's nature's way" was something Dad said all the time. It was "nature's way" if rainwater splashed over a sill; "nature's way" if somebody fell from a rooftop; "nature's way" when you skinned your knee and it started to puss over. "Nature's Way" was a malignant humor that could not be managed with a smile and an umbrella. "Nature's Way" was something that called not for eternal vigilance, but absolute resignation. It was the snare that caught the bird; the net that drowned an alewife; the thunderbolt that burned your house down to a crawl-space for stray kittens.

"Go on," I said, "fly away."

I put it back where I found it and dashed away. I wouldn't go back there for the longest time. I didn't want to see or know what had happened. One thing was certain, however; I had, without intending to, made a statement; left an impress; walked away.

"Problems," said my school friend, "make us who we

are. I am a Problem, and so are you."

Remembering that little bird, I said: "I'm not a problem. You take that back!" I gave him a little shove, the kind you give when you're throwing down the gauntlet but don't necessarily want to fight.

"I don't mean to offend. I was just—"

The next shove toppled him.

"No need to do that."

"You take that back!" I said. "I am not a...problem. How can you say I'm a problem? You don't know. You don't know anything about me."

"I thought being a problem would be of comfort to you," he said, from a crouch. He wasn't done trying.

"Just leave! Why did you come here? Why?"

Dusting himself off, he said that he was sorry to have introduced such a idea; that maybe I was an exception to the rule; and that perhaps he had spoken out of turn. He wanted to make amends for this rash thing he had done to me. There were people in the world, he said, that weren't problems; they didn't have to be anything at all. Then I told him that I wasn't upset about my dad anymore. Me mum had made it all right. I was perfectly all right without him. I didn't need him. Not really. All I needed was for people to leave me alone.

"I'll do that," he said, walking away. "You looked sad to me and I wanted to know why."

"But I'm not, you see. I'm not sad at all. See?"

What did I expect him to divine from the newly constituted persona I had, smiling from ear to ear, constructed? I guess I wanted to leave him with a good impression. Perhaps he might want to befriend me another time. I knew, however, that I couldn't be perceived as a negative quantity, a problem among so many others—a bleeding heart that might overflow. As he went away, I wanted to run after him and tell him everything. Yet in the end, I refrained from moving in any direction. I became as stock-still as I had ever—or would—become. Perhaps I had seized, without knowing it, upon that fallback position which, when we screw up, braces our fall and gives us the illusion of a second chance. I knew one thing: I didn't want to be singled out for something everybody might well have, but shouldn't have to own—certainly not to a perfect stranger. I've never liked well-meaning persons. I suspect that they might pity me and, while I may want a touch of it, I'd rather be in control of it myself.

Yes. The purposeful calm that *he* had exuded all of those years went right to me mum. I'd never seen anything like it. When she instructed me to see his killer, she could have been asking me to check for the paper or find her purse.

How this relates to my own destiny I can't quite tell, though I don't believe all that twaddle about avenging a father, whom I now understand to have been weirdly sanctimonious. No child likes to consider his parents as sexual beings, but I think the absence of sex is a lot worse. It made me mum almost crazy. If there's any parallel between my loathing of what old Bruce represented and her feelings for my father, it was in the condition of her eyes when she contemplated him in his chair. It was unpitying, ineradicable, and totally malevolent.

I've got one more thing to say about them, then I'll move on.

They staged a little soiree one evening, after some sort of dining experience they rarely allowed themselves. But someone had come over and persuaded them to join her. They were all part of an informal Resistance during the War—a resistance that cleaned up after the planes went away. There were bodies to find, children to look after, and chaos to comprehend. Or, if not that, to hope against hope that the Spirit of England had not deserted everybody overnight. And would not until Our Ordeal was over.

I didn't hear what had happened at this restaurant, but

I was, as usual, shadowing them. I learned to be invisible during those years, the amiable cipher who pops out now and then; the precocious observer who knows when to use his napkin and when not to; the fine little lad who wears his breeches right and doesn't make any trouble that doesn't find him first.

A neighbor called Dumfree, a Scottish refugee, had brought something to drink. (This must've been a bit of a strain, coming after the dining experience into which they had poured all of the ragged civility that wasn't extinguished at home. Or maybe they just invented it on the spot. That's what she was good at doing. He was fatally sincere, with just a dollop of imagination—just enough for him to be able to see a table with figures and apply them to the responses that would be socially necessary. That's what he did with the railroad, look at tables and do things with them. Every man who punches in at the office may not want to get out of it, but he might consider the toll he takes, just by showing up, on his fellow men and women. I doubt if Dad ever had such a thought. He liked to think of himself as useful, and those tables gave him a handle on it.)

Yet the War was a great unifier. Every block had war clubs, death-and-destruction sodalities—followed, in peace-time, by gab-fests and get-togethers that permitted a virtuous generation to discuss all it had done, not only to keep body and soul together, but to re-stitch the fabric of a country one needle-stroke at a time.

"Excuse the mess, if you please," said me mum, directing Dumfree inside. He was followed by another stolid-looking creature that stopped at the door, as if whatever was within might poison her.

"Come on," said me mum. "I'll turn on the lights. Then we can—"

"Have us a little drink," said my dad, who had never said anything quite like this before. Was this the ever-reliable, eminently untouchable human being who had been so callously fair, so irreducibly reasonable?

"You go in there," he said to me mum. "You go in there and scramble us something. Something we can pick at as we're reminiscing over various and sundry things that are dear to us."

I'm quoting him exactly. He could say things like this and seem perfectly natural, as if he himself could embody, any time he cared to, the Spirit of England.

"I don't think we have anything," she said. Then she waited a beat or two and announced that she was joshing them, like some sort of American mother that had a car in the garage and lots of canned food in the cupboard. "I'm just pulling your legs. I can yank something out of a hat with the best of 'em, I can!" At which she wobbled a bit toward the kitchen and turned on the stove. Why she turned on the stove she probably didn't know. It was like boiling water for an out-of-hospital birth. It made you feel better about something that could go well, but might get out of control and keep going.

"Look how it glows in here," I heard her say. "Come in here and let's turn out all the lights. And let's contemplate this little gas-ring."

"No more rationing with those," said Mr. Dumfree, at which the missus unaccountably laughed.

"Nope. We're all clear now. We can have as big a bonfire as we want," said my dad, who seemed to be getting into the spirit of things. I'd never seen either of them like this and I was so mesmerized that I didn't care whether I was invisible or not. I needn't have worried. They were so preoccupied with their little fun that, as long as I lurked in the shadows (of which there was always an abundance, even with all the lights and burners going) I'd never be noticed.

"My dear," said my dad to me mum, "you can make something for us to nibble on. Here in this repository of domestic bliss. What is a kitchen but...but a place for all of our values—everything we love most about our beautiful lives—to come together and knit us into a community!

Just like we were with all those bombs coming down and Hitler grinning at us from his bunker, or wherever he was at the time.

"Hitler made a real impression on me," said Mr. Dumfree.

"Yes, he did on me too," said my dad, who looked genuinely happy.

"Well, then," said me mum, "go into the parlor and I'll bring it out when I'm done."

They all filed away, tooth and comb, into the aforementioned room, where I would, so many years later, go through everything they had and keep so little of it.

I was closer to the kitchen, where I settled down for my vigil. Mum was also happy, in an ankle-length dress that didn't quite sweep the floor but didn't show her ankles either. It was the sort of dress for people who had settled as opposed to taking the bull by the horns. But me mum had shed all of the eyebrow and forehead of her loathing, that scrunched-up area of the psyche which was all about tension and eschewed release. She'd become the girl she'd been before she married. Before she had me. Before everything that had made her so obtusely bitter, so single-mindedly against, rather than for, anything.

And what do you know, but Mr. Dumfree came into the kitchen looking for something.

"D'ye have a match?" he asked me mum.

"I believe I do," she said, producing one for him.

"Yes, I believe you do," said he, looking her over in a way that struck me as too-familiar.

"Go on back. I'm going to get you all something you haven't had in a long, long while."

Mr. Dumfree, who was a large person but carried himself like an athlete, scooted over to where she was, as if he would block any movement that might occur out and away from him.

"Let me go by," said me mum in a conciliatory voice, followed by a fluttery laugh.

"I like the look of you going by like that," he said.

"Well, I like doing it, so I guess we're in agreement."

Said Dumfree, closing in: "Oh, I think we could be in agreement in all sorts of ways."

"I'm sure we can," said she, doing a little twirl around him. "I'm sure we could in *almost* every way." Her emphasis on the word *almost* had a teasing quality, as if she could take or leave the joke.

"Yes, that is what intrigues me," he said, without moving into her. He seemed assured of a conquest he might not have even thought about, coming into the kitchen and asking for his match. Yet, from my observer's perspective, she appeared, by discouraging his advances with her tongue, to be encouraging him in the way she pranced about. It wasn't so much embarrassing as disturbingly unfamiliar. Here was this woman who looked like me mum doing things I'd not seen her do around Dad.

"Come here to me," said Dumfree.

"No, Mr. Dumfree, I don't think I'll do that."

"Then I'll come to you."

When he did, she held out a single forearm, as if two were one too many, and said: "This can't go any farther. I'm a happily married woman."

"No, you're not," said Dumfree. "I can tell. I can always tell."

"Be that as it may," said me mum, "you can't be making overtures."

At which he drew her to him and kissed her as passionately as people did in the movies, where, when I went by myself, I saw people kissing more passionately than the silvery shadows on the screen. At first she struggled, but changed her mind. I could see it in the way she moved into him; pressed her hips to his; kissed with an audible smack. I was hopelessly fascinated to see my vengeful mother melt as she did.

"Oh, the burner," she said. "The burner!"

At which both of them came to their senses at once.

"You go into the other room," said me mum.
"Yes," said Mr. Dumfree, "I think I should do that."
"Yes," she said, "I think you should do that too."

I heard me mum and dad arguing that night, but she got the better of him. To his protestations regarding purity, she told him to fuck off. That's precisely what she'd said. "Fuck off," she told him, nearly ten years after the bombs had fallen and England might have been frayed into little Nazi camps. It was our solidarity, that rich and sumptuous quantity, which had pulled us through. That and our airmen, who had been shot down by the dozens, but were able to do more damage to them than they could, with their bombs and such, do to us. As Churchill had said, never had so few done so much for so many. And so a nation survived to tend its gardens and have rancid meat for dinner. In the persons of me mum and dad, it had been breeding right along, as if wartime provided the best possible excuse for propagating the species. And they had me. And decided, unilaterally, that I was too precious a thing to permit spousal sex. Yes, unilaterally. Which is why I never said anything about what I'd seen. I had a sense that she needed Mr. Dumfree's overtures, even if she would never go any farther than she had that evening. Moments after he left, my dad came into the kitchen and said he was glad that friendships made under the most terrible circumstances were the most enduring: yes, after the ravages of war, the ritual of re-adjustment, and the reconstruction process in which every man jack could participate if he or she wanted to. (In this context, women were men too. It was war and everybody was a potential victim and therefore the same. At least in one's fairness-leaning imagination.) The important thing was that the War and its aftermath had deepened ties that might have otherwise come undone. Then he left, saying, "Mr. Dumfree, I want to shake your hand."

At that point, me mum did something that made my

hair stand on end. She took a utensil from an unseen drawer and threw it, as if the window were a target, straight into the garden. She threw it so hard that the glass she had broken was only faintly audible. I'm not exaggerating. I just heard the whiz of the thing, which was as wicked-sounding as any bomb.

11

*W*hen Mum died, I had to face the reality of being an only child, which is to lose all family connections abruptly and for all time. No brothers or sisters to share your burden, just sour memories of beef and cabbage; forlorn birthday candles stuck into white frosting; loveless looks exchanged across an uncrowded room (we never had visitors—except for her parents, who didn't care for the flat or the neighbors or anything else. And, of course, never came back. As if to emphasize what a great life they were having and somehow underline the dearth of greatness in our own, they sent us Christmas cards that could've been made by Charles Dickens himself. The best and brightest of everything. Yes, their sleigh-bells rang clearer, their snow had fewer urine-trails, and their Santa Claus's were fat, but not hyper-tensive. The only time I ever visited their house in a pleasant village for which I'm glad I have no name, all the tinsel hung just right, there was fresh mistletoe over the doorways, and smiling faces— smiling to beat the band—faces that didn't succumb to flashbulbitis when the bomb went off. The surprised look of so many people of that era came from having their features sucked into an electronic explosion. You should see some of mine—though I'll never show them. No, not if they pay me five million pounds for the book I know everybody will want to read. (Or maybe not: O. J. Simpson's pseudo-confession was, as I remember, withdrawn.) At any rate, we were put in our place and they stayed in theirs.)

Next door, if I may digress, was a little girl named Evelyn. She was my second family. She was the one who came over with the cookies me mum failed to make; showed me coloring books with pictures of Superman and other *Ubermensches;* took me out of myself with pantomimes that involved damsels in distress—whom I would always save. She was the one who, on a sad occasion whose cause I can't remember, held my hand and whispered tidy little encouragements, such as you say to the hopeless or deranged. I once tried to molest her—if that's the proper word. She simply waited for me to stop, as she knew kindlier instincts would prevail. Even then, she embodied some kind of moral force that would ultimately find the better angels of my nature. And, oddly enough, it did.

As I was clearing out the house, she re-appeared.

"Hallo!" she called into our old living room. I'd messed it up quite horribly, with odd-sized boxes, packing-tape, and my recent obsession with orderly process—which looks worse than chaos until everything's all done. By that time, I was working in a shop. We specialized in furniture, though we'd get the odd painting, a bit of chinaware, that sort of thing. It was called Clew and Sons, though there was only one son and didn't ever seem to be another. Perhaps it was the paterfamilias' wishful thinking that had created the extra son or sons. I would never know.

"Who's this?" I asked, genuinely curious as to the identity of this new and more than reasonably attractive person. I'd pushed past forty by the time—which was about her age.

"You don't recognize me?"

My mind flashed to those clubs we played. Some girl I'd picked up for a bit of fun? I hadn't a clue.

She was very nice looking, in a kind of middy blouse with heart-sprinkles all over it. And a slouchy hat I had always identified with lady-gardeners. Her slacks are what caught my eye. No bulges or bumps. No straining thigh-tissue or adipose bottom. She was clearly in some line of work that favored a good shape over a bad one. An airline stewardess? Hostess in a club? Maybe she worked for one of those Bond Street art dealers who came into the shop now and then with a sheaf of bad watercolors. Or a down-at-heel Sir Henry Raeburn from an estate sale that had gone awry.

"You really don't know, do you? Shall I give you a hint?"

"Failing instant recognition, I suppose that would do."

"Before we get into that sort of fun, please allow me to offer my condolences. I liked your parents, though they were rather distant people. Well, their generation was like that."

"Yes, I suppose it was," I said, not wanting to disagree with somebody I should have known but could not fetch away from this sparkling creature who had just come to brighten up a few moments of a long, long day. The estate agent was supposed to come, but had to cancel. There was also a litany of workmen who needed to tighten knobs, pound in floorboards, and freshen up all the nicotine-colored paint in a house with no smokers. (Dad put the occasional cigar in his mouth, but took it out after a few puffs. He couldn't bring himself to enjoy as little pleasure as that, the lunatic.)

"All right, then. What about us sitting in here and you trying to play doctor?"

"I played doctor?"

"And very well, I should think. If we had ever been stuck in an old house, you would have had your boyish way with me."

I couldn't remember playing doctor with anyone here. Unless it was...

"Evelyn?"

"Took you long enough!"

I tried not to lunge at her, but that was my compulsion. I realized, then and there, that I hadn't been with a woman in a full year. One should acknowledge such things by fits and starts, if at all.

"I can't believe it's you. You're...you're..."

"Over forty," she said, amused at my groping for language.

"I wasn't going to say that. You look ten years younger."

"You don't look so bad yourself, sir."

I almost blushed at the compliment. People who crave attention, as I used to, are often shy about receiving it. When we were onstage, I took it for granted. In fact, I got to be quite arrogant. All I had to do, if I knew some bird was looking at me, was give her a kind of after-work-is-over nod and she'd show up at the stage door.

"I walk a good bit. Don't stay at the pub. Eat my Wheat-a-bix. You know."

"I would like to know even more. I know you're busy, but what would you say we take in a little entertainment tonight?"

"Uh...I guess that would be all right."

"Good. As it so happens, I've been blessed with theatre tickets."

She shook her purse as a guarantor of these items.

"Well, let's do it, then. Where shall we meet?"

She gave herself the opportunity to ponder the question as adorably as she could. She even took her index finger and let it splay out along her cheek, as she attempted to contemplate a range of tantalizing possibilities.

"Why don't I just come back here? Have anything to drink?"

"Their stuff—Mum and Dad's."

"We should be able to rustle up a few drinking glasses."

"Let me warn you," I said, "the liquor cabinet was never filled. I think there's one bottle of the worst Scots whisky known to man."

"We won't stay here, then. Unless you have something else in mind..."

I rose to escort her out of the house.

"No, my dear patient of yore, I regret to say I do not for the time being."

Which was a lie, of course. When she left, I was in such a rutting condition that I had to "off" myself in the shower. Those psychologists are so right. After pleasure, guilt sets in. Then the search for pleasure again. Then self-recrimination, self-loathing—which has often led to self-help, which I absolutely despise. When we do something shameful, we should have shame-inducing mechanisms to put a dampener on future impulses—which can make them all the more desirable. Did me for a while. Checks and balances. He said, she said. Right and wrong. Without that, the moral faculty would wither and everybody would run from everyone else. Just as many of us are doing now.

She picked me up an hour before curtain, but we decided to walk. The spring-like air (anybody notice how parents choose to die in the spring?) was invigorating as she took my arm, as if we were in a London Fog advert. However, it wasn't quite spring yet and, as dusk settled over us, she nestled closer. I was wondering what I'd done to deserve such luck. I was doing all right at that point, having "transitioned" from a not-so-eager prole to the desk-jockey your true proletarian pretends, or wishes to, despise. After my record was given to a specialist in employee aptitude, I was given a job at the shop. And thus I was finally whisked—though hardly in due time—from the knockabout aspect of my business to its silken interior. If I never sit in another lorry, I'll be all right with that.

It would be disingenuous to say that I deserved the job. During the interview—which was full of "standard questions"—I was able to pick so many of the right answers that I *was* whisked away from my lowly station and brought upstairs. By the time Evelyn came into my life, I had breathed that rarefied atmosphere for a matter of months. It's surprising how quickly I assimilated the place—which is to say its principal mores, at the top of which sat loyalty to the firm. The curious rectitude of my fellow minions was as strained as it was superfluous. Most of the "fellows" were the genteel-living poofters who were always complaining about their mums. One of them, who called himself Sinew Fantod, asked me, on impulse, why I didn't care for mum-bashing. I said that me mum was a pretty good sort. It was my dad that had fucked me up. After exhaling as mightily as he ever had, Mr. Fantod left the area, never—at least on my watch—to return.

"Get anything accomplished?" asked Evelyn, with a little clutch at my arm.

"Dribs and drabs."

"What will you do with all of it?"

A lorry-driver was getting dangerously close to the curb. I felt an urge to stop him and explain the niceties of traffic safety. If it had been raining, he would've splashed us. Of course, I'll admit to such hooliganism myself and have only the dimmest of excuses. I was young, etc., didn't know what the hell I was doing. And, oh yes, I'd been betrayed by a poofter who had wanted to kiss me in a public area and—lest I've a hankering to forget—been drummed out of the world's most successful rock and roll band.

I suddenly turned morose. She tugged at my sleeve as a way of getting my attention. With little success. I can be a great Nietzschean bore when I want to—even when a delightful young woman has decided to latch onto me.

"Get you down?" she asked. "Well, we're going to a comedy. That'll get you right back up."

"I suppose," I said.

"No doubt about it. I don't mind telling you that I've taken a whirl at the psychiatric profession."

"You don't say?" I said, with no consuming interest in this "whirl" of hers. Yet I found it strangely disarming. I sometimes wondered whether I hadn't sneaked out of "analysis" prematurely. Perhaps it would have shone a light on the frazzled recesses of my psyche and somehow prevented the murderous messages they eventually sent.

"I was horribly depressed a few years ago."

"What about?" I asked, settling into our little walk. The West End wasn't terribly far away, but we were taking it slowly. The shops, with their spill of lights; the traffic, which bobbed and weaved around us; and all the brightly sad and sadly intelligent looks of day-workers coming home: these conspired to weave a little spell whose attractions were not inconsiderable. Here I was with Evelyn, the little girl next door, walking toward an adventure I couldn't, drunk or sober, have anticipated. Clearing out my mother's house was one of the most dispiriting things I had ever done. And here Evelyn comes into it, with brightly colored veils, a brisk outlook, and a penchant for psychiatry.

"Oh, this and that. Look!" she said, pointing at a bus. "The Keysters have re-united and are on tour again. I thought that last one would kill them."

"Oh, yes, I see."

"Don't you like them?"

"They're all right."

"All right! Where have you been? They've taken the entire world by storm. A second time! If they hadn't come to America, our benighted cousins would think of us as tea-addicts and Winston Churchill clones."

"I know all about them."

"So much for international diplomacy. I see you're more of a domestic type."

I looked over to this woman who had emerged from

primped curls and cute dresses and was duly ashamed of my knee-jerk morbidity.

"I'm sorry. I suppose I'm down on everything."

"It happens when you're obliged to confront the endings of things. That's one of the reasons I sat on that formidable-looking couch on Harley Street."

"Oh, yes," I said, as a way of finding the present.

"Oh, yes indeed!"

She stopped and I stopped with her.

"Before I share those traumatizing experiences with you, perhaps we should have a spot of something."

"Perhaps we should," I said, leading her into a little place that was small and steamy. In those days, you sat at tables with strangers—or did in a place like that.

She took a chair at the first table we saw. An old bloke sat at the end of it, with his head stuck in a newspaper. I saw the word "détente," which petered out into a sea of grey. He nodded to us by way of acknowledging an invasive species.

"Hello to you too!" said Evelyn, more for my benefit than for his.

Somebody came by with a pad. Just showed up. No word. Just a somewhat disagreeable human presence.

"What'll it be?"

"Tea for the both of us, please."

"Nothing else?" she said as a way of reminding us that we were occupying valuable real estate but not contributing much to the rent.

"A few scones."

"What kind?"

"Any old kind. Just throw some apple jam on the plate and we'll lap it up around them."

"I'd be glad to," said this lump of sour beef and went on her way.

After we settled, Evelyn reached across the table and wove her fingers into mine.

"Now tell me about your reaction to that

announcement. It strikes me as a more pressing matter than my psychological programming."

I hadn't told anybody about those times—not past that lorry incident. (I don't include my public outburst, which was essentially anonymous. It got some attention, but it had no color, no reach, no story. It could have, but I chose not to tell it.) I knew better than to throw my disappointment around like a rag doll. Nobody likes to hear about failure—even if it is imposed from the outside. I'd say *especially* if it is. It's offensive to the British strain. It says that no stiff upper lip can prevail against the vicissitudes of fate—an unendurable affront to our character! It says that man is a victim—which we, as a nation, proved with all the firebombs exploding around us that we were not. And it seems to suggest that you, the so-called victim, have no say in what happens to you.

She listened intently and without apparent skepticism. If I was recruited from that nasty club, so I was, then. I had a good singing voice and a stage presence that was very agreeable. When I talked about Salzburg, she didn't suggest that I was dreaming it. She believed that the Austrians were taken with us, that we didn't sleep, and the fresh-faced girls of that nation enjoy being spoon-fed pastries before and after bed.

"And so they dumped you," she said, concluding my story in her own words.

"In a word, yes."

"Well, I think that's about as traumatizing a thing that can happen. Your talent was minimized, your contribution to the group went unacknowledged, and your manhood was in shreds and tatters. I'm sorry to seem glib, but I'm completely sincere. Small wonder you're not an alcoholic. Uh, are you?"

"No, no," I said. "That would be too predictable. Besides, I don't care much for pub-sitting."

"You could have taken it home by yourself."

"I loathe my own company."

I meant for that to be a joke and she took it as one. I was thinking that this Evelyn was the breath of fresh air for which I'd been yearning, but was not, until this moment, aware of it. I suppose when one deprives himself of such air, the fetid stuff that gets into his nostrils feels like the real thing.

"You don't think I'm a disgruntled, disillusioned madman?"

"Not a bit of it. You can be morose, but that's understandable, given the incredible secret you've been living with."

"Well, now it's not."

"And high time! You can't live in the present if you're re-living the events you described to me."

"No, I suppose not."

Came our scones, with a slather of something that might have originated in an orchard and might have been prepared by some chemist with a malevolent sense of humor.

"Oh, look!" exclaimed this all-understanding creature that had swooped me up and said life was possible. "They forgot the scones!"

And they had. We'd been served a plate of buttered toast.

12

I suppose my time with Evelyn was the happiest I've ever spent. Looking back on it, I marvel that the bitterness that stayed with me after we broke up could be greater than the sum of our love, affection, attachment, and whatever else accrues to one's character as a result of being lifted out of the worst part of it and finding the best.

She never seemed to mind that I'd, to my mind, failed and had accepted something that was *just good enough*. And yet, I had a gift for understanding the often-small, precious objects I handled, labeled, showed, and, on many occasions, persuaded other people to buy. The great era of televised expertise had not yet begun, yet I was beginning to become quite a star in the firmament of disposable income.

My boss called me in one day from the counter, at which I drummed my fingers until someone asked me to remove something from a glass case or small strongbox. Then there was that suspenseful moment during which the predator's eyes went dead or glistened surreptitiously. If the latter occurred, I'd close in and begin selling the object, whose attributes may or may not have appealed to me. I suppose I liked closing in for the kill. I could almost liken it to the transformative moments I derived from smacking a hoop of varnished wood against my thigh and intoning words that seemed threaded into me like beautiful little vapors. Yes, I could almost do that, but it would be a sort of sacrilege. Fact is, there was—and is—nothing to replace a feeling like that. The way to get through life is to go at something else that might be just as good.

"I've been watching you," he said.

"I hope to your satisfaction," I replied.

"Oh, yes. Yes, very much to my satisfaction."

Mr. Clew (nobody called him Roderick) was a stoop-shouldered fellow with a tawny-bearded face. His accent was hopelessly impregnated with the vowels of Manchester—where I think he spent a lot of time as a very young man—which he attempted to shore up with London everything else. He was a peculiar combination of youthful buoyancy—though he was already in his fifties—and stodgy *sangfroid*. You never knew whether he was going to get excited or slip nearly into a coma. It was one of the joys of working with Clew and Sons. The Clew in question was very much the second man, though the father was alive somewhere outside of London. Clew Fils referred to him as "The invalid". I never found out whether the elder Clew was an invalid or not. It was clearly none of my business, even if Clew the Younger was always trying, by means of ahems and innuendoes, to induce me into playing a guessing game. Strange, how even the moderately powerful think the less powerful are hopelessly captivated by the piddling details and middle-grade minutiae of their lives.

"In point of fact," said Mr. Clew in one of his excited phases, "I have plans for you."

"I'm glad to hear it."

"Come into my office on your break and we can discuss your future."

I showed up an hour later and told the young lady at the desk—whom I would see coming into the store, but never going out of it—who I was and what I was about.

"Just one moment," she said, punching on a big telephone.

"A Mr. Asunder is here to see you, sir."

I could hear a "Send him right in!" and rose to meet the voice. She was having none of it. While in mid-stride, I was told that Mr. Clew was expecting me. Which meant that he was expecting me and nobody else. That meant I should wait my turn—in spite of the fact that nobody else was in line. Or would be. Yet, as I advanced, she assumed full-block position, like an American footballer. I have often wondered how somebody who makes a minimum wage can muster such loyalty. She was probably infuriated with my cheek. She wasn't allowed to express such a thing, so why should I be?

"Thank you very much!" I told the girl with a mock gratitude that rang out as falsely as I wanted it to. And continued walking.

Mr. Clew's office could not have been anything other than that of an antique dealer's. Gilt and ormolu sparkled from soft maple varnishes. An old clergyman looked as if he'd been caught, behind his motley-carved frame, in mid-sermon. More than one layer of oriental carpet cushioned one's footfalls. The room itself was antique, from its enormous pocket doors to its somewhat frightening chandelier, which looked too heavy for the choke-hold of the ceiling above it. The ceiling itself seemed light years away, as if the Victorian model of the universe had somehow prevailed and the world looked up to plaster moulding instead of stars and galaxies.

"Please, pull up a chair," said Mr. Clew, who rose with deliberate care and sat down recklessly.

"Thanks for calling me in, sir," I said. "I recognize that it is an honor and a privilege."

"Tut, tut," he said. No one had ever said "Tut, tut" to

me before. I had the pleasurable sensation of appearing both in my own life and in an old movie.

"What I want to discuss with you is the notion of a partnership. Not the usual kind, which involves blood and primogeniture, but an intellectual one, if you will. You have a uniquely comprehensive grasp of our stock, whatever it may be and during whatever time you may be handling it. I've rarely encountered such a smoothly adequate appreciation of the netsuke mentality."

"Just a matter of boning up. Go to the library, sit awhile, and you've got it."

After standing by a work ethic I'd never considered much above average, I said: "Never was one for flash-cards and such. I sit there until it sinks in."

I was going to say that it was better than being a lorry driver—if not quite as satisfying as making records that spanned the globe and would keep spanning it as long as there were needles and turntables—and whatever else has evolved from them. Now, of course, you don't have to buy anything. Go to the Internet, download something and you've got hours—even weeks —of listening pleasure. The Keysters wouldn't have made it in this day and time. Shows you that certain phenomena are only possible at certain periods, that there's a window for them, and if whatever needs to slip into it doesn't, that window closes for all time.

"Such industry is hardly average. I know. I've burned a good deal of midnight oil myself. Yes, even as all the others slipped away."

If he'd been lying, his paraphernalia gave the opposite impression. On his enormous desk, among the letter openers and framed snapshots, was a whale-oil lamp, with long wick and blown-glass container. I put it at around 1850. I hoped the subject would come up so I could show off a little.

"I see a lot of me in you, and vice versa."

"I'm very flattered, sir."

"No need to be. I'm, as they say in those gangster movies, leveling with you. Fact is, I need someone I can rely on. I need someone who's not only steady, like Pauline out there in the front, but someone who is acutely aware of the business. Oh, I don't mean balance sheets and all that. I mean the poetry of it. Yes, the poetry! Does that surprise you?"

Though I shook my head, it did surprise me. I suppose it was more than a job to me, but I never thought of it as a vocation. Even then, I had the refugee mentality. I was still, in my view, hiding out. Perhaps we all do it to a certain extent. Unless we're lucky enough to be in a big rock band and be able to suck the oyster out of its shell on a daily basis.

"No, sir, it doesn't. Every business has its numbers—its linear stuff, if you will—but you'll also find, in the daily practice of it, in its draggy little routines, some semblance of a divine order."

Mr. Clew clutched his heart as if said organ were giving out, but it was not. It was merely full of a joyous affliction. He couldn't help but get up out of his chair and race over to me.

"To hear you say that is...it's absolutely thrilling. You've put in a nutshell all my heretofore unarticulated philosophy. Let me shake your hand."

We clasped hands for a little while, during which I wondered about Mr. Clew's sexual proclivities, seeing as how I have traditionally attracted the poofter element. And yet his squeeze was purely platonic. He was simply overjoyed at my (as he understood it) understanding.

As he skipped back to his desk (he was in an energetic phase) he kept muttering, "Yes, he's put it in a nutshell. In a nutshell indeed!"

The upshot surprised even more. A substantial raise, my own office, and access to people I would see, like Pauline, coming and going, but never spoke to at any length.

Though I'd been cast aside by Jake, Townsend and Marshall, humiliated by Peregrine and put to rout by Bruce, I was accepted in this musty little world into which one could slip like a mite or insect and burrow in for the rest of his life.

Yet I believe I'm getting ahead of myself. I want to talk about Evelyn, with whom I would eventually share a little flat. I've been dreaming about it of late. It wasn't charming, but it didn't need to be. She was there every night and that's what made it not only bearable, but essential. I never thought I'd experience love (or what have you), but there it was between those curtains and bedcovers and the street, which seemed very far away when we were doing something—anything at all—inside.

If I had lived alone, its undistinguished contours and rasher-smelling doorjambs wouldn't have done anything for me except what places usually did. Once I was in them, I wanted to leave. Something in me resisted putting down roots, gouging hoof-prints into a floor, having a newspaper come on a regular schedule. Until later on in life, I'd always picked up things as I needed them. In that regard, I think I was living like young people often do—ready to leave piles and messes as they sprint away. Having come into the business, as my mentor would have it, I became more interested in the leavings of others than what I might drop along the way myself. When I met Evelyn, I was in the midst of a house-cleaning that was so brutally expedient that it took my breath away. I'm sorry I didn't save the letters me mum and dad exchanged during their courtship. I remember his hand, gaunt and leaning, getting the worst of a windy day. Hers was nothing of the kind: straight, tall, and somewhat intimidating. Like an architect's. It was as if she knew who she was and he was settling in behind her. When the tables turned after I came along, I had to re-assess them. He was the assertive figure—or at least the dominant one—and she the little pressure-cooker that boiled over now and then. I know I studied her lists for the grocery, but I don't remember them being startlingly different. Perhaps they were. At the time, I wasn't paying that sort of attention.

Yes, I wish I had saved a few of those letters. Might have interested the War Museum. When the bombs rained down, so much of our heritage was incinerated. Whole blocks of peoples' lives up in smoke, rendered down, become antimatter. Most of the vacancies that were fairly common when I was coming of age have been filled. Like you put in new teeth. Or slam a book onto a table, except that, when you build a house, it's going to stay for a while. Or that's the idea that possesses people when they build something. Perhaps it's our vanity. How much of Shakespeare's England exists today? Yet there must've been homebodies who couldn't have been much different than we are. Clipped the hedges, tisked at all the rose petals when they floated away, worried about the porosity of thatch and wattle.

Yes, I wish I had saved a few of those letters.

Some months into our relationship, before we decided to live together, Evelyn and I met for lunch. She'd been working for an airline and had been somewhere exotic. She'd brought something to shake at me: something that was crudely made, but clearly authentic. My appraiser's eye bore holes into it, but my lover's mentality prevailed. Because she offered it, or was perhaps about to, its value was, to me, beyond monetary considerations. And its metaphysical status was infinitely greater than it could have been on a display-counter in a trinket-store.

"I got you something," she said, sliding next to me. Her favorite scent was on, which evoked a smallish garden somewhere in the country. I drew it in discreetly. Later on, I hoped I'd be able to see it suspire from her pores and skin, then lick it off them. I think my ardor embarrassed her initially, but she would eventually come up to it herself.

"What is it?" I asked, shaking the little thing.

"It's an idol of some sort."

"An idol, eh?"

"Yes, you pray to it and it will grant you every possible wish."

"I fear it is too late. I already have mine."

"Why not have an embarrassment of riches?"

"Why not indeed?" I said, shaking the thing the way a baby might shake his rattle.

"Not like that!" she said, taking the thing from me. "You've got to really shake it. Like a tambourine! You see?"

When she said tambourine, I froze, though I tried not to let on. Of course, when you're stock-still about something—which is a strange sort of attitude for living tissue—somebody will eventually notice.

"What on earth is wrong?" she said, rubbing a hand that had gone stiff on the table.

"Oh. Nothing. I just...nothing."

"Oh, no. This is something writ large. You must tell me or I'll go get a physician."

I really didn't want to drag the past into our reunion. It was always so much fun meeting her somewhere and listening to her go on about a foreign country I'd never heard of; outrageous exchange rates; dictatorial regimes that would kill their own citizens but welcome travelers with ticker-tape if they knew what in the hell it was. No one had ever opened up to me like that. Of course, I hadn't encouraged it. You might even say I repelled such confidences. This Evelyn was the antidote I was unconsciously seeking. She dragged me back into the present, from which my work—which focused on expired things—and my waning obsession with betrayal and intrigue had taken me far away.

"It's really nothing. Please. Let's not go into it."

Before I clammed up, she jerked us out of the restaurant and onto the street.

"If this has something to do with that singing group, you've got to fess up, my dear fellow. If something must come between us, you should at least have the courage to tell me about it."

We sat down on a bench near St. Paul's, whose deep-tongued bell I could hear at the office—not that that was special. All of London could hear it. I'd been up in its gallery and listened to my voice drop down past the choir stall and the pulpit deep into the earth, where it gathered strength and kept going on and on and on. The acoustics there put every other place I knew to shame.

"When you said I should beat it like a tambourine, well, it brought those old days to mind. I did that, you know."

She moved away from me, not because she was put out, but because of the revelation she was about to share.

"I found a picture of you playing it. At some club in Austria, I think. It's there. You really did it. I must admit that, in the beginning, I thought you might have some grandiose idea about what you did, but found, in that picture, that you did not. I want to apologize for not believing you. I mean, not completely. Not as a lover should."

"Did you, then, mention the tambourine deliberately? I mean, as a way of drawing me out?"

Somebody walked by and jarred into me. In the English manner, he apologized.

"That's all right. I think my leg was sticking out."

"Yes, it was," the man said. "But I should've been looking."

"At any rate, I accept your apology."

"That's a good fellow," said the man, who might have just gone about his business, but did not. He had an axe to grind and, because it had been given special emphasis by our encounter, he wanted to share it. Then and there. He warmed up to his thesis as a clergyman might, with a little sneeze and a swatch of handkerchief, with which he mopped perspiration from a domelike brow.

"You know, courtesy is passing out of the world. It happened with that rock group, you know, the...the...well, never mind who they were, but they sowed the seeds of anarchy into the world, which is, in my opinion, reeling from it. Yes, reeling. Well, good day, sir. And you too, milady."

"Yes, same to you."

"You can't catch a break, can you?" said Evelyn.

"But I have," I told her. "You're sitting here with me."

13

*I*t was at about this time that Jake had his major meltdown, as it is known today. The Keysters' last album, *On a Harley Street Afternoon*, was almost ten years behind them, all the members—even Marshall—were doing their own projects, and fortune still showered its fruits upon them. Bruce's efforts had become saccharine. Without Jake, their tinsel nature bloomed, though they did all right in sales. Bruce's work sold because Bruce did it. And because of Keyster nostalgia. Whenever people saw his face on an album cover, they could dream of their own youth; remember young girls leaping and swooning; and think of those same girls—once Keyster-mania had left their systems—losing their inhibitions in the backseat of a Plymouth Roadster. That sort of thing happened here as well, but more discreetly. Though infected with the new malaise, English girls and boys still had a spot of Mum and Dad. I'm not sure what the statistics on pregnancies were, but I'll bet you they were nothing like they were in the U. S. But each in our separate ways, we had ceased to identify with our parents. First Elvis, then the Keysters, were linked to the social revolution that induced young men to present National Guardsmen with a perfect daisy. If truth were known, political passions were no preoccupation—at not least in the days when I was around. Asked whether social conditions in England were any worse than in Norway, the lads hemmed and hawed.

"Where's Norway?" asked Townsend.

"He doesn't know where Norway is!" spluttered Jake.

"Do you?" asked Marshall.

"Of course I do. While you gits were passing messages around, I was concentrating on me geography."

"So where is it, then?"

"Norway is on the six hundredth latitude, and bounded by Mother Russia to the South and the Great Cambrian Ice Flo—spelled like the lady—way up above the Land of Skyblue Waters. That's where Norway is."

"So he does know it!" said Townsend guilelessly.

"I think we should check that out."

"You do it, then," said Jake. "It's just where I said: Norway, the land of perfect yellow teeth and snowshoes that fit comfortably in a reticule."

Jake was in Los Angeles, being rowdy for the most part, and making records for fun, as he infamously said. His exact quote was: "I don't do Keyster hits anymore, but I'm having it off and I'm loving it!" This with a long-armed salute, as if he were tossing a final *bon mot* from the gangplank of an ocean-liner. In one fell swoop, he managed to ridicule his old band-mates, put to rout any notion that work could be serious, and affirm that having the time of one's life was the best bloody move one could make.

He would convene a press conference somewhere and fall down. He was always doing that, partly for the sheer stuntsmanship of it, but also because he'd developed, in semi-retirement, an alcohol problem that other people in the business found boringly retrograde. With all of his money, it seemed like he could have done better than swig domestic beer and lean away from any camera that was put in front of him. Noticing the popular brand he insisted on carrying into an interview, a brash young man who would make his name in public broadcasting wondered whether he, Jake, had not returned to his working-class roots.

"Never shed 'em," said Jake, ostentatiously proud of something he mentioned hardly at all. With houses and apartments all over the world, and with royalties materializing by the millisecond, it was rather hard to identify with the Sunday-in-the-park, lunch-on-breeches sorts he used to sing about.

"I see. So you like this sort of beer?"

"Sure. It's what people in Cleveland and Milwaukee are drinking."

"Yes, I would imagine they are."

"You said that snidely. What do you have against Cleveland?"

Jake posed this question with a mock belligerence, puffing himself up like a lord and daring non-existent buttons to pop out from his shirt-front.

"Nothing, as far as I know."

Jake came around and, as mobsters say, got into the man's face.

"As far as you *know*?"

"Yes. If you don't mind, sir, could you possibly, uh."

"I could possibly do a lot of things, you young whispermapper. You daughter of Dido's dimples. You gridiron grommet!"

In order to catch his breath—or lose it entirely—Jake took a massive swig from his can, belched, and started afresh. In a parody of gracefulness, which he accomplished by means of stutter-steps followed by tightrope-style careening, he treated his interviewer to some on-the-spot choreography.

"I will twirl about this lamppost singing in the rain." (At which he sang, badly, some snatches of that song. Being averse to all forms of respectful adaptation, he substituted the word "singing" with "wanking" and kept it up for as long as Gene Kelley had.) "Yes, and I will leap across this lovely bit of grass for you. And, to prove that I'm a solid, one-hundred-percent degenerate, I will sing "Tiptoe Through the Juleps" at the top of my lungs and in a gorgeous falsetto. (Which he also did, trilling lubriciously.) "You know, I said I'd only sing for money, but that was when I was just a wee lad and hadn't enough of it. Now that I have money to burn...here, I'll show you."

Jake took the interviewer's cigarette and put it out against a movie poster. Having forgotten to make his point, however, he found it, lit it again, and rummaged in a front pocket for some bills, which came out in a bundle. He stooped to pick one up and applied the cigarette to its combustible center. As he tossed it away, he said: "Catch it if you can, O wanderer, catch the little dollop that will make your day!"

A lean and hungry person complied and scurried off, not only with the burning bill, but with a few others that had tumbled out of Jake's pocket. The interviewer eyed them, but he was too image-conscious to pick them up.

"Now, what were you saying?"

Having seen that money can go up in smoke—something the man would have never encountered in his profession—the stupidly undaunted interviewer asked Jake a burning question. *The Keysters had broken up. What was the possibility of them patching up old wounds, saying their apologies, and getting back together again?*

"My dainty fellow," said Jake, draining the can that had ceased to be conversational fodder. "Dost know of the snowball, which, when in hell, doth melt?"

Given a beat to answer, the interviewer could provide no insight into the question.

"I'm glad you know of it. But what of the tinker's damn we give to things we don't give a hoot in hell about?"

A producer had ceased to hope for an abrupt, but face-saving, conclusion to the interview. His gag sign was not, however, acted upon. Perhaps Jake had seen it and wanted to escalate the situation. In life, one thing generally leads to another; it was fatally irresistible in this interview.

"You must know of that one. Everyone knows a tinker. And if he doesn't know a tinker himself, he knows of someone who knows a tinker. And so on. Yes. And so on *ad infinitum* the curtain is down and the village is being sacked by stewards and shuffleboards. *This is the BBC, everyone, and I want to tell all of you what a delightful program we have for you this evening, featuring a tired-out old rock band fronted by a pedophile and given musical depth by all of his minions, who are only occasionally curious about under-aged girls.*"

By this time the interviewer had started to gather up his things, which consisted of a little pad and a microphone for himself and his victim. His movements were somewhat jerky, as if he were having a hard time remembering how to finish up with something that always came to an end. Yet he managed to get everything together and started moving away. The palm trees parted alongside him while a smog-shrouded sun shone onto a highway that looked like spun glass.

"Hey," said Jake, following him. "Don't you want your knuckle sandwich?" This in the style of Humphrey Bogart.

The sensible man kept marching off to a better day.

"No? Then I'll give one to myself. Now, isn't that stupid, for a former teenage idol to give himself a bloody nose? It's downright masochistic, that. But you will oblige me by turning the camera this way and recording the incident for the world to see and reflect upon?"

The cameraman obliged while Jake battered himself, minding the nose, but giving his cheekbones a nice little bruising.

"That actually hurt, you know. Well, let no one say that the British Empire does not produce courageous sons. No, we stood up to the Hun, I don't know how many times, until we got frankly tired and, instead of producing stout-hearted fellows, we spit out decadent little rock musicians who wanted to shake like Elvis, but ended up looking, frankly, like librarians. I can go into this bar over here and drink copiously to the good people of Cleveland, Milwaukee and...Chicago. Yes, city of big butts and shoulders. Butts mostly. Yes, nice big Polish butts you can shake a stick at, and I can too. Now where is a stick?"

The cameraman followed Jake, not to a stick, but to a waste-bin, through which Jake rummaged like a prop-master who's been directed to find a tea-set, but comes up with a metronome instead.

"Not that," said Jake, with many pardons. After extracting a newspaper whose headlines he showed, sheepishly, to the camera (they said something about a recent debacle in Vietnam), Jake marched round the waste-bin as if it were a decorated soldier.

"I'm sorry, ladies and gents, to be obtuse, but I have this marching fever inside of me and cannot help myself. Will it expire? No, not as long as there is breath to trumpet the triumph of our great men—no women to speak of, just men—in the military. No, it will not expire for as long as patriotic feelings swell my breast—would you mind getting a close-up of my breast, cameraman?. And, finally...finally..."

Like a car that suddenly runs out of petrol, Jake began to droop. As he lost footing, he held onto the sides of the waste-bin, which wobbled like a coin somebody has tossed onto a floor.

"Please forgive my indisposition," he said, as a cockney lady who belches loudly and has the delicacy to know she shouldn't do that. "Yes, please do. I'm just a poor little girl who's trying to make a living over here with her flattened bosoms and scrawny little legs. Just a poor little girl who needs to get medicine for her mother and maybe a bit of chocolate for herself. Not much, just a little drop in the mouth that'll sweeten her dreams for a while. That's all. In the meantime, ladies and gents, I think I'll just lie down here and...don't mind me. To this fate, we all may come.

Unless we can screw our way out of it. Did I say that? I'm so sorry. It must be the heat of this new city, which quite unnerves me. Yes, it does. It quite...it quite..."

The cameraman was prescient enough to not only record Jake's splendid monologue, but keep it to himself, claim the rights to it, and sell it, many years later, to a Keyster's archivist for a quarter of a million dollars. "Jake's Million Dollar Meltdown" it would forever be called. It's all over the Internet now. I saw somebody watching it on the Tube—what Americans would call the subway.

I was shocked, but not much saddened, to hear of his *piece de resistance*, which happened days after the interview—and the one I had with Mr. Clew, which would set me upon a vastly different course. That evening, after Evelyn and I made love, I told her what I'd seen on the television. Because she didn't know whether I'd go off or not, she didn't want to mention it.

"Yes, I heard. Very sad," she told me.

"In LA. I wish it had happened here."

"What does it matter?"

"LA has no character," I said, twirling my hand in hers, which was tacky-dry. It had me on it, and her—mostly her, really. I'd licked her skin, her pores, and everything else with flesh on it and had released her personal odor, which was like a fine little biscuit with some apricot on it. I once told her that she smelled better than a boutique with dried eucalyptus and twenty-year-old salesgirls. She seemed not to think it far-fetched, but blushed in that very seemly way of hers. Some people can't blush. She could, and it was so endearing I can hardly stand to think about it.

"He's gone. What does it matter?"

"Dignity. Old-fashioned values. I would just have preferred that he went here."

"But not in the way he did! Better that it happened over there."

I looked out the window. Our street was never placid, but its noonday roar would decline, during the night hours, to an agreeable hum. When it rained, cabs and lorries hissed up and down it. Double-decker buses found deeper grooves, releasing a finer music, a hum that hummed inside of itself. I couldn't remember, until I met Evelyn, listening to anything in nature—or what we have of it in the city. My ears had been corrupted by recorded sounds. It was as if—after I'd watched those records go round and round—the audio-scape of life wasn't turned up loudly enough.

She got up for a moment, possibly to let me look at her, which I liked to do. Nothing is sweeter than contemplating a physical form you have just ravished and has ravished you. My eyes roved her body with a familiar sense of its bourns and boundaries. After dwelling on conventional perfections, they found the miniature sinkhole at the small of her back. When we were lying down together, I'd twirl my fingers around in it until she started laughing and begged for me to stop. I'd never known a girl who was so ticklish. Or could be reduced to teary-eyed laughter after a less-than-dedicated assault.

I stuck to my premise, which seems, in retrospect, *outré*. Why did I care so much about Jake's dignity? Or the practice and preservation of home-country values? The Keysters had helped shatter them—or had at least given them a good whacking.

"Sometimes you're so very...British," she said from her perch by the window, in whose sill she sat. She looked like a living goddess who had been misplaced in Kensington. The hard surfaces that supported her—sill, window-seat, and floor—looked hopelessly symmetrical, like small ships caught in a storm at sea. Sitting there, she seemed to say that Life Triumphant was sticking up for itself in this room and wasn't going anywhere.

"And you're not?" I asked.

"In a way I am," she said. "I'm sorry, but I like the way these bands have opened things up. I know you're bitter about what happened, but, whether you carried this spirit into the world personally or not—I know it matters to you and it should—it's a good thing that it got there. When I was a girl, things were a whole lot stuffier. I mean, there wasn't any talk of having fun. It was all duty and 'having died for the crown'. You see what I mean, don't you?" she asked, slipping back into bed.

"I see that you've decided to join me again."

"I can't stay mad at you for long."

"I don't believe I ever could. I mean, be mad at you, let alone stay that way."

"Then, what do you really think? You can tell me."

"About Jake? Well, he had his moments. And it wasn't really his doing. He was just part of the...cabal, spearheaded by that stupid poofter."

"He meant a lot to people, especially during that horrible war."

"I know. I was proud of him in a way."

I sang the best-known verse of a song that is cropping up a lot these days.

> *Take the low road out and the high road in,*
> *We're not goin' back to where we've been;*
> *People all over want us to say*
> *Let's all recover from the American way.*

"That *was* effective, wasn't it?"

I needn't have asked it; it was so effective that America denied old Jake his passport. He countered by writing *Keep the Newsboy Out, but the Barkeep In*. Not much of a song, proving that one should not speak out in anger. At least until it settles down in the craw. Jake had a lot of it himself, but, to his credit, it came out sideways, in what Townsend called his "jabberwocky". To do them both credit, I'll have to agree.

"I believe it was instrumental in stopping the war. I believe it was," said Evelyn, whose eyes had begun to tear.

"Don't cry. Please, don't."

"I can't help it. Something just came over me."

She went to get some tissue, at which point I knew I was damned. I wasn't at all sorry about Jake. He was "one of them" and they'd left me out in the cold. It didn't occur to me that Evelyn was a part of this icy waste I thought I was in. Or that I was moving toward a fairly comfortable, away-for-the-weekends sort of life. No. I just said what popped into my mind. Which, as I understand now, was the beginning of the end. I'd even thought of marrying her if she'd have me, but the occasion never quite came up. It did in the sense that such an occasion must be seized rather than dreamt about, but I suppose that's always been my problem. I don't do things. I react to them. Oh, but I did something then. Or, rather, I said it—which is sometimes one in the same thing. I think everyone has a little dish of bad words he or she wishes to take back. I wish I could take back the words I said before she leapt up out of bed, threw her clothes on, and stormed through the door. Because she'd never done that, it not only shocked me in a general sense; it shocked me *into* something. For those lucky (and uncomfortable) few for whom consciousness is a daily practice, well, more power to them. For most of us, it is a temporary condition, relieved by a mostly unconscious plateau over which we limp from one kind of fuzziness to the next. What did Shakespeare say about greatness? Some get it thrust upon them, some achieve it, and some...I can't think of the other. When she left, I became conscious of one thing leading implacably to another. One minute, I was twining my fingers through hers; the next, she was scrambling into her clothes and exiting as if someone had shouted "Fire!" in a theatre. To this day, I wish I hadn't aired my true thoughts. If I'd not said I was somewhat happy that Jake had stepped onto La Cienaga Boulevard on the wrong side of the street—as we British sometimes do in America—and been run over, it is eminently possible that Evelyn and I would have a nice little country place in the Cotswolds, full of bird-watching and homemade wine. Some nice neighbors, though not too many. Fog in the morning, but clearing nicely toward the afternoon. And dinners at a crook-in-the-road, where you could warm your feet by a roaring fireplace and hear the latest gossip, which has the worn and comfortable piquancy of good round words that have a nice sound to them, but don't mean anything personally. Just a lot of white noise to take one into an evening of considerate lovemaking and a soundscape created by all of the things that fly from eaves, rise up from dead branches, and keep the world moving when no one and nothing else can see it.

Yes, a nice little country place that's denied those of us who manage never to live in the present completely. For that, we are sent to the back of the class, to the corner of the potting-shed, to the very end of a line we joined early on, but decided it was too straight, too long, or too shabby.

14

*T*he joke has it that Marshall was—and is—such an uncharismatic person that, if he died, nobody would notice. So, when I shot Bruce, he was still there, just not exerting a great deal of influence—though of all the Keysters, he was the one who most supported me when I was with them and most denigrated Peregrine for the little bait-and-switch he did with me and Bruce. "You shouldn't knock Vijay. He was wildly vocal. I mean, his singing really stuck to a person. I'd be out there banging on things and I'd hear him over all the cacophony, if that's the right word. Yes, the cacophony. Which he civilized, you know. For my money, he was a lot better at the mike than either Jake or Bruce. And Townsend, well, he was strictly for joining in after it all started. Nothin' wrong with that. Just that he wasn't, you know, out there."

Yet for all the time that elapsed between Death Number One and Number Two, he was fairly visible. His studio-assisted, heavy-on-maracas album, *Friends of Theirs*, made a respectable showing, mostly because of its personnel. There was Craggy Bettlewhite on guitar, Stoss Helving doing his thing on various keyboards, and the incomparable Jesus Quintana shaking all the stuff I used to and a helluva lot more. When you're of a mind—and have the money—you can hit the charts with almost anything. As he said, "I threw it up, hoped it stuck to the wall, and it did."

As to his views on Jake's traffic-oriented demise, he exuded the magisterial calm of a seventh-degree black belt warrior (or seasoned bartender).

"Jake," he said, "was his own man to the last. 'Course, he could've looked both ways. 'S'what me mum told me. Turns out, she was right."

Marshall doesn't—and will not—figure very prominently in this chronicle, but I wanted to mention him as a kind of paperweight to my story. He was always there, he liked me well enough, and, in spite of his barely-visible status on the great celebrity graph by which we calculate the comings and goings of our betters, he helps anchor the reality that began to unravel once the Keysters were no more and calamity struck one of their members each decade following its/their demise. First there was Jake, then Townsend. I shouldn't say decades apart. It took Calamity fifteen years following the curb incident in L. A. to find Jake. Townsend came almost hard upon, and not from any accident—or at least so it was described. Two Keysters shouldn't go as if they were lousy Keystone Cops, so Townsend's mortal coil had to unwind with more gravitas—even if it probably didn't. I never got the true story and don't really care. Aside from his guitar, Townsend was, for me, a completely negative quantity. In their first movie, they buried him, a non-reader, behind a newspaper. In the second, they took middle-distance shots of him in his swimming trunks, looking as Ichabod Crane might have in similar attire. Yet he was given some of the quirkiest lines. In the first, some smartypants asked him for his opinion about astronomy. After establishing, by an upward glance, that he knew what astronomy was, he said: "It's rather too planetary for me. I prefer the good green earth, where we plod out our days and make honeyed music." That was more like something Jake would say, but Townsend spoke it as if he were fully capable of such philosophic blather and enjoyed springing it on you like a bad joke.

All in all, it took me thirty years to screw up my courage and find Bruce exiting from his favorite Zen garden and plugging him there.

Didn't mean to let the cat out of the bag. Having done so—and believing it to be obtuse to undo anything so casually indiscreet, not to say downright manipulative—I'm going to scoot ahead to my thralldom to the antiques business, in which, as I said, I had accomplished such inroads. And would come to enjoy, insofar as I could *enjoy* anything. Such a simple word, yet for those who can do what it suggests, there's a lot of life to be drawn out of it.

It was in Mr. Clew's establishment, some weeks after Evelyn broke out of our embrace and sought the comfort of thirty thousand feet over various continents, landmasses, and oceanic graveyards, that another figure from the past came walking in. I'd decided not to poke around my office that morning, but mind the store, as one might say.

I particularly liked the cabinets that had occupied grand, but now-humbled, establishments all over England and Europe. Some were agreeably various, with nooks and partitions; squares and cylinders; varnished wood alternating with smudgy brass. In their midst, I hardly thought of myself as an expert, but a gamely clueless explorer, a man without a country, a kid, as I liked to say over and over, in a candy store.

"Very nice, aren't they?" said a tall gentleman.

"Very nice indeed," I said, primping my collar and swinging round.

He was clearly interested in these wares, but also in me. Another poofter, thought I. But from years of dealing with the sons of gentry, not to mention my own brush with the breed, I was ready with elegant repartee—or sophisticated bawdiness, if that was required.

"Have you a larger one?"

"A larger what?" I asked suggestively.

"One of these, of course."

I'd taken the wrong tack and righted myself.

"What are you furnishing, an airplane hangar?"

"I am not. I'm merely wondering whether these represent a certain limit, beyond which one may need to have one made."

I went over to the biggest and caressed it. The old car ads in which lissome lady experiences a small orgasm when mounted, as it were, on the hood of a car from which she mimes the masturbation of any protruding element were the gaudy counterpart to the kind of salesmanship at which, I will admit, I excelled.

"Please accept my apology for making light of your ambitions. In Clew and Sons, there is room, not only for the physical component of things, but for the imagination as well."

"Hmmm," he said, walking around the biggest piece. "Hmmm," he repeated, as Englishmen who did not want to betray an indecisive strain in their natures did at the time. Now that Empire is gone and people aren't as class-conscious as they once were.

"This one might do," he said.

"It is a handsome piece of workmanship and has an impeccable provenance."

"Where was it, do you think?"

"It says right here, sir. Shall I read it to you? Not to accuse you of illiteracy—or even spotty eyesight. I'm just here, I have my glasses—I daresay I need them as much as you do—and, well, I'm ready to begin."

He was a tall gentleman, but his features were small, as if the genetic qualities that brought him to his height had gone into retreat when they expressed themselves in eyes, nose, mouth, and forehead. He tried to dress jauntily, but it was not his nature. He should've dressed as formally as a body could get by with in those days, which was a formidable leap from what's *de rigueur* nowadays except at the most posh affairs. He should have also had someone with him: a retainer or yes-man, somebody who would pay attention to his every beck and call, though not to the point of actually doing anything.

"Go ahead, then," he said, finding something in a pocket and twirling it round. A nice touch if he'd been in the right outfit.

"Let me see. Oh, yes. Print's rather small. Should I leave out a word or two, I hope you'll forgive me."

"Just the gist. All I want. You know, where, when, and, uh, how much."

"Of course! I'll skip all of these allusions to Crystal Palaces and such."

He jerked the thing in his pocket, but was otherwise unperturbed.

"Just the essential fundamentals."

"Just those."

Peering around the corner, I saw a man whose presence I had been secretly dreading all these years, knew I'd eventually have to reckon with it, but felt safely out of reach most of the time. I'd hardly thought about him at all, really. Aside from that brief incarceration following the impromptu performance I'd given in the aerie of that enormous theatre, I hadn't seen hide or hair of him. But there he was, eyeing a bit of shelf. For the prissy stuffs he liked, no doubt. I had a momentary vision of him putting them there and shook it away from me—though discreetly. It would have been seen as a minor twitch, something one had to deal with, the kind of cross ordinary people must learn to bear.

"Go ahead," instructed the customer, whose height appeared to increase in the midst of those strangely miniature knobs and depressions which enlivened his disproportionate face.

"Yes, of course! Constructed for the event whose name will be shorn from the record in 1847, this multi-compartmented cabinet resided in the British Museum until the early 1950s, when it was taken out of wartime storage and put at auction."

"That's interesting."

"Not really. Museums are always deaccessioning things."

"No, I mean the..."

I heard nothing the man said for Peregrine's sudden prying. He had seen me, but didn't want to let on. But he was creeping in his way. Creeping ever closer.

I saw my potential quarry nod a bit, and then peer into the curved glass, which seemed the perfect counterpart to his transparent—though not altogether straight-up-and-down—sort of nature. I let him tap on it, though that sort of thing was generally frowned upon. I didn't care what he was doing anymore. I was thinking only of Peregrine, the architect of my fate, who was hovering around shelves, but knew how to creep. And kept creeping...

When the man asked me whether he should write a check to the establishment—or was there a private broker?—I instructed him to wait for a moment. *This customer over here, you see, has been wanting to ask me a question and I feel, in the interest of the excellent service we tender at Clew and Sons, I should go over there first. You don't mind. Good.*

"Hello, my dear boy!" exclaimed the man whom I hated above all men in the world. I certainly hated him above all men who were male-oriented.

"Spying on me? Want to clap me in leg-irons again?"

"An unfortunate incident; I wish you'd just come to me."

Peregrine was sporting a cane. He liked to swish it around, not as a military accessory, but as a kind of probe. It could contact hard reality and relay its message. An unyielding surface was to be avoided; a well-padded one might be better, but hardly ideal; while an over-cushioned, fluff-impregnated one was absolutely perfect—provided something harder-featured might enhance it later on. His face had thickened a bit and his eyebrows were turning yellow—not an attractive yellow, but a bone-white that's been stained. His pudgy little hands stuck out of combed silk while his tottery legs glommed onto the floor like bloated pincers. You never know how much you hate someone until it comes to describing them. I could never paint Evelyn's picture except in the most sacerdotal of terms. About this lump of jellied tissue, I could not write a congenial line.

"And what on earth would I have said? Or could you have said? How can you rationalize something like that?"

He sighed openly, like a man who was asked to contemplate a tragedy that's peripheral to his everyday experience but might well consume a sympathetic nature that is always on hand.

"If you'd just listen! Why don't you meet me somewhere and we can talk about it?"

"If you'll notice, I'm conducting a sale."

"Oh, with that gentleman over there..."

"Yes. He'd be the one."

"Well, then, I'm going to have someone deliver this piece to me. You can take care of the sale or not. But let us meet this evening. I'm thinking of, well, no, not Punjabi, that would set the wrong tone. Tell you what. Why don't you get off work and call this little number? We'll decide where we might want to go then. In the meanwhile, you're looking so fit. You must jog or something. I'm afraid I can do nothing with myself. But, then, I've never cared for physical culture. Unless it happens to someone else."

I watched Evil take its time exiting the room, as if its suspirations would linger. Then I returned, with many apologies, to my customer.

"I hope you'll forgive me for talking to that man over there. He was very impatient and wanted to know everything *now*. You know the type," I said to my first customer, who was getting to know his future acquisition very well. I caught him looking underneath it as I talked to Peregrine. It never occurred to me until that moment that he might have been a dealer himself and was "playing" me. If so, his play was reasonably fair and I didn't mind getting the worst of it. Sometimes a "colloquy and a commission"—as the elder Clew liked to say about near misses—were enough to satisfy the inner man.

"Looked all right to me. Dresses a little fancy."

"He does everything like that."

"You know the man?"

"Only his type."

"What type am I, then?"

"You're forthright, not easy to impress, a good man to have in a pickle. Battle of Britain."

"Saipan. Got nicked up pretty bad over there. Well, it was for a good cause."

"Yes, it was," I said. "Our generation was made possible by you fellows."

"Some of us. I was in supplies. Did nothing but deliver casks, gunnysacks, and oddly shaped wooden boxes."

"The honored dead of our country. The very people who have made our emerging prosperity a fact and not a tittle. Great anonymous, flag-bearing fellows who went into the fray with only one thought in their heads: To preserve a way of life like no other. No, like no other in the entire world!"

"Lord, no! Olives. That sort of thing."

"Oh," I said, with the deflationary accent of the grandiose-having-fallen.

"Don't care for them myself."

I got back into the swing of things with barely a missed beat.

"I like them in a martini," I said.

"Filthy things, really. I remember one of the boxes leaking. Stank up the whole plane. Give me the occasional kipper, but it still reeks of where it comes from. I like things that come from the indoors. Always have. Filthy things, olives."

"As you say, sir. Filthy."

15

I thought about taking the low road in and high road out, as Jake had written. But I was not in a high-road taking mood. I felt embarrassed, humiliated, double-crossed, blood-up, and not a little curious. I hadn't heard much of Peregrine since that night. I learned, after I was let out of jail, that he had, somewhat too conspicuously, paid my way out. I never knew of his conniving nature until I heard about this well-tuned generosity, which would play in the press and emphasize my lunacy. I sometimes wondered, sitting at my desk, when the younger Clew would come in, identify me as the raving lunatic who had commandeered a televised interview, and send me packing. But he merely smiled upon seeing me at my invoices or training another salesman. And it was just that: a smile and nothing else. It is only in literature that see-through people bore us. There's no greater boon in life.

Peregrine had written his number on a small, pink slip of paper. I was surprised at its neutral smell. Seems like Pouffy would have succumbed to his predilections more publicly and passed scented notes around. Or kept a little tablet that exuded essence of lavender whenever he took it out. At that point, he didn't need to hide. He had so much money that he could buy his way into anyplace he wanted. England was no longer about what escutcheon you had on the wall, but the color, texture, and magnitude of the stuff in your pocket.

I called the number from a pay-phone downstairs. My heart was hammering as if I'd not only been running, but running away from something. I was the man who had dogs coming from behind and shooting-rifles leveled at their victim's progress.

"Hello there!" said Peregrine, divining my presence somehow.

"You wanted to have dinner somewhere."

"Sit somewhere. Have dinner somewhere. Doesn't matter."

"Doesn't to me either."

"Well, let's have dinner, then. Wouldn't hurt. Unlike you, I can always be hungry."

If he'd been closer, he would have thrown back his little head and touched my wrist. Hilarity of his sort requires contact.

"I've thought of the very place. Discreet, but nice to look at. Well-known, but not quite enough. And full of interesting people you really don't care to meet."

"Fine. Where?"

"I wish you'd relax. We'd have a much better time that way."

"I'm not interested in good times."

"You're much too intense for me. I'm surprised you're not Italian. Your name is Indian, of course, but you have nothing of that horrid accent. Sounds a bit like Bruce, if truth were known. He's asked about you. Well, now I'll have something to tell him!"

"Where?"

"Where? Oh, where is the restaurant? That's easy."

He rattled off the address with the fluency of an in-crowder. It had a funny name. Deliciti. As in *corpus*. No, as in *flagrante*. Of course. His turf and not mine. Perfect, as it always was. For him anyway.

I got there at the same time he, Peregrine, did. I recognized some people from the press. They were fleeting profiles and familiar-looking bodies scurrying into a club. There was a pop star from our era, shaking a new haircut at a perfunctory suitor. (This suitor had the pleasantly possessive demeanor of people who have always gotten their way in life. He might have been thinking of the lovemaking he could stop and start at will—or some other activity he might lazily dominate.) The song for which she is better known now—thanks to the internet—than it was when it was released popped into my head. A pretty little brainless number, full of glittery people and staying up all night. The sort of thing the Keysters were good at for about six months. From that time on, they became increasingly dark. When the journalists first noticed it, they predicted a precipitate downfall during which an adoring populace would reject their frightened spinsters and dispensable paperbacks. But the journalists were always wrong. The darker Jake and Bruce got on the page, then inside of the studio—with its full range of bizarre, but appropriate, bells and whistles—the better everyone liked it. I sometimes wonder what would have happened if Elvis' content had become multi-layered in the way the Keysters' got to be. I don't think he could've pulled it off. He was just a hip-shaking country boy without the complications of history in his head. The Keysters were something else entirely. And the same idolaters who had embraced Elvis would embrace them too. I couldn't understand it. And still don't, really.

Delicti was, as Peregrine said, posh, but not top-of-the-pop. It was the sort of place second-tier celebrities gathered to contemplate their assault on Tier Number One.

He came over to me as if we were old friends. In fact,

he slipped his arm into mine and used it to steer me over to "our" table.

"Do sit down. And let me order a glass of wine for you."

"No, thanks."

"Please join me!" he said, letting me go. I rustled inside of my jacket, conveying a sense of acute discomfort. Expressing revulsion in a restaurant is never a good idea.

"All right, then," I said, surrendering not only to the tony atmosphere, but to a more powerful, albeit silly-ass, person's mandate.

He did not beckon any waiter. The one who found us slipped into our airspace like some sort of dark matter with a bolo tie. All the waiters wore them. They said: "We are not trying to project the image you think we might care to." Which would become delightfully confusing once the wine bottles stacked up and everyone was in an accepting mood.

"Get us something red. And fruity. I prefer blackberry notes myself. What about you?"

"I prefer wine," I said, making my joke but deriving little pleasure from it.

Peregrine threw back his head and let out a gusty something that resembled an elephant's orgasm—or what I would like to think of as one. Our waitperson was momentarily embarrassed.

"As we all do," Peregrine managed to squeak out. "As we all do indeed!"

The waiter left. I sank back into my chair, which was harder than I would have thought a chair in a place like this might be.

"I don't care for the seating either," admitted Peregrine, though he probably had vastly different reasons for regretting his chair.

"It's all right. I'm not going to stay that long."

"Oh, dear," he said, looking over to me like some refractory pupil who will never get his lessons, but has some sort of arcane promise. Parents are trying to push him to go into the family business while all he wants to do is write sonatas. Or play about with pea-jackets and fishnet hose.

"Look. I'll make no secret of not wanting to be here. And with you in particular. You know what you did and I don't think there's any making amends for it."

Peregrine leaned over, with his two pudgy hands clasped in a heartfelt way, which he proceeded to place above the area where that organ would normally reside. I can, in retrospect, feel inordinately delighted that this man, whose heart had, to my mind, vacated his body, would be struck down by its refusal to endure beef-tips and Bailey's Cream Ale. Of course, there were those other creatures. Perhaps he succumbed to zoophilia and a heart attack in one fell swoop. That would put his demise in the same gaudy regions as his life—or the life he might have led had he been the savage opportunist in it as he'd been with me.

"I'd never want to do that. You see, you were a victim, not of any malice on my part, but of an image I had one night. Yes, I was sitting at my desk daydreaming, you know, and I saw the band as I knew the world would eventually see it. And you were not in that picture. Think of...Mount Rushmore with one of those lesser presidents. I know it's painful to be likened to such people. And I don't mean it that way at all. No, indeed. You were the group's very best singer. What you did to 'Sweet Georgia Brown' was so indecently thrilling that I've kept every version of it to myself. In fact, I haven't released any of those tapes to this day. Perhaps it's time. Something we might think about, eh?"

I tried to demur. I didn't want him to ease himself into a high road he had never taken. Yet the opportunity quickly passed. He, Peregrine, struck the table—in his way. Nothing jumped up as it would have if an ordinarily emphatic person had done it, but it was so uncharacteristic a gesture that it got my attention.

"I *never* changed in my assessment of your talent. Never. No, not even unto this very day."

He wanted me to be grateful, but I wasn't. Such a confession fell into the "too little, too late" category. I was able, for a moment, to co-opt an aura of righteousness and revel in it completely.

The waiter materialized in a material fashion.

"Thank you!" exclaimed Peregrine, who let his glass be filled. I told the man I'd pour my own.

"As you wish," said the waiter, mortally offended. What, he seemed to be thinking, can't I pour well enough now?

I've never understood how people do a job like his. Always sucking-up, being attentive to whims and caprices that have not yet been spoken, and living with the daily humiliation of being rated by smarmy gratuities. You might say that my job entails some of that. But because I like—or, rather, liked—the stuff I sell, I don't mind the "by-any-means-necessary" approach. I'm not always throwing low balls to my clients, but when I must, I lob them in and they're hit precisely where I want them to be.

"Have one. Let's just sit back and enjoy our time together."

I envied such serenity. Peregrine was truly right in his mind and soul—insofar as he had one.

"If you could only take the historical approach. No. Given your place in it, that would not be suitable. But try to bear with me. Would you? Please?"

He gave me the sort of dreamy look that is embarrassing when photographed. If it were being provided by a contract player, there would have been batting eyelashes, a coy retreat, and some clinching laughter. Yet the look faded out into something rich and strange—as if he'd hoped to be able to use it for quite some time and knew that the time had, at long last, arrived. I was moderately disarmed. Here was a man speaking through his heart, sclerotic an organ as it had come to be.

"You, of all people, should understand what destiny is. Well, there was a kind of destiny in the choice I made. Once I saw that image, I had to arrange things so that it would be replicated in real life. And so it has been—though I was mortified to learn of poor Jake out in California. So ineffably talented. And spokesman for one noble cause after another. A warrior for peace and yet a peaceable one, as it turned out. Of all of you, I think he was most morally centered—yes, even more than our Bruce, whose exploits on the ice absolutely flummox me. I mean, how much more does the man have to prove?"

He'd forgotten Townie, but he'd never become a cultural icon. He was just a guitar player with chops that were envied by artists as far-flung as Judy Collins and Jimi Hendrix. Peregrine was a Big Picture sort of guy for whom the details, having been assembled correctly, might fall where they may. And for the stuff none of the lads could do, Villiers was there to provide the fancy bits and half-monte's. Needless to say, there was no need to drag Marshall—whose charmed life was as lively a topic as his years with the band—into the conversation. He hovered, as he had during the Keyster years, outside of it.

Peregrine paused to daub lips that were ruby-coated.

Now, what was I saying?"

"You were talking about Jake and his moral center."

Oh, yes," he said, with that confidential air again. He scooted closer, though there was enough of him in front that the table stopped him before he got too close.

"You know," he said, looking around like the possessor of a Great Secret the world must wait to hear, "I thought the Dalai Lama incident was big, but he kept on topping it and topping it. He never had to do that, you know. It was him and that slut of a Chinese so-and-so he married. I so preferred the other girl, whatever her name was. Her waning film career has, alas, become a subject of much immediate, if transient, interest."

My mind flashed to the woman he was talking about:

an attractive blonde whose name, for some reason, escaped me. She was the girl I would see coming in and out of the club. Always with a book. And scooped into those pre-spandex outfits. I'd never seen Capri pants filled out in quite the way she did. Her flanks personified that quasi-beachball, pear-shaped quality painters have been at such pains to reproduce. Rubens made 'em too plump. Modigliani elongated his tits and ass to the point that they looked geometrical, which is the worst thing you could say about a woman's attributes. There's a great picture by Giorgione. It's of a naked woman surrounded by two blithering swains who are completely clothed and making no bones about it. She's there to be looked at and, at some distant point in the day, taken by one and all. Old Giorgione knew what it was like to smell the steam rising up from an oozy bottom. He had the sensualist's jump on the anatomical, which was so delightfully organic that there's no separating body from scent; legs from torso; a diamond earring from The Divine. I've gotten to know painting, from the job I do, pretty well. If I hadn't gone into music, I would have dabbled about with oil colors created, for amateurs and professionals alike, by hyphenated craftspeople. I would've sat out an ordinary workday with a model holding a pose for me, then taking a cigarette break such as the working world had never seen. I would have given art lessons and married one of my pupils. A redhead with bones I'd want to study during the daytime and jump at night. A schoolteacher who didn't mind plunking down safety and stability in the service of Art. A politely profane creature with a winning smile for opening night and bawdy repartee for when the good people go home and it's just us bohemians sitting around with a hard-on and a hash-pipe. They say art's relaxing, but I have a feeling it's not. If Chaim Soutine were ever relaxed, I don't think he'd have been able to stand it. Or Frans Hals, who gesticulated his life away. Or any number of gits we contemplate, with intelligent chin-strokes, in museums and wonder why we can't be as happy as they were.

Yes: I'd always liked her voice and wondered what it would have been like to wake up next to her. "Vijay," she might have said, "you surprise me no end." Or words to that effect. I could have never written pornography. I can't quite screw myself (as it were) into the right epistemological position. Huh. I've never used that (*epistemological*) word before. I'm not even sure I know what it means. But I know what it meant to see that girl whenever I came and went. Christine. No. It wasn't Christine. Sometimes all you can remember is what something or someone isn't.

I poured a bit of wine for myself. The bottle must've been quite expensive. It had those fruity notes Peregrine wanted. I studied this bottle, as if it were an antique property—which it almost was. It had the usual chateau on it, whose nomenclature was being "controlled" somehow. And whose vineyards had, from the year in which the bottle had been released, been straining to produce more wine for increasingly jaded appetites and shrinking expense accounts. The world is rich and various.

"That's right. Just settle back and we can have the philosophical discussion I really wish was possible back in the day. You'd have such serenity and acceptance now. Anger. It kills us faster than cholesterol. Or poverty. Or a string of bad marriages. You must purge it from your soul!"

This from a man who had every reason to know, and practice, serenity. I read somewhere that his personal wealth was estimated to be in the billions.

"I am not—nor will ever—be serene," I almost said aloud, sitting across the table from a billionaire who, in a more frugal period, had wrecked the life and hopes of a man he had "discovered" in a small club and presented to three slouchy-looking guys in the back of a semi-detached house that had been spared by the firebombs that rained down from the cargo bays of Nazi fighters.

"Would you care to order anything? Needless to say, it's my treat."

"No. Nothing."

"How's the wine?"

"Good. Fine. Something to sip while you prattle about destiny."

"Have you been to therapy?"

I didn't want to admit it and would not.

"Hell, no!"

"It might do you some good. If you care to pursue it, I can give you some names. I was in it for a while myself. For vastly different reasons, of course."

"Of course," I said, watching the former pop star take the hand of her millionaire and squeeze it. With that little operation accomplished, she probed a bit more deeply. The location she'd found was evident in the look on the old man's face. If you can be startled, overcome with lust, and still reasonably functional, this old man was all of these things. I envied him his capacity for pleasure as well as the status that had made it possible. Even when I was with Evelyn, I couldn't throw myself into a full embrace. I always lurked somewhat outside of it. When a shadow comes across your path early on, you keep walking into it.

"I don't need therapy."

"Don't kid yourself. We all need it. If Gandhi could have done it privately, he would have gotten it."

"Not me. My feelings have always been crystal clear."

I gave him an unpitying look, charged with such malignant urgency that Peregrine actually blanched. Being of the high-color persuasion, his cheeks were as ruddy as a summer apple. When I leveled my look on him, the color went out like a lamp. For that moment, he had become the carcass he would in his casket, with artificial blush, pallid lips, and a swept-clean forehead. No hair on his face, which looked fully scrubbed and pathetically infantile. If it were not for the stark terror in his eyes, as well as the vestiges of the resourceful intelligence that also shone there, he could have passed for a mewling child. I thought he might actually become ill.

"I suppose therapy can't be appropriate in all cases," he managed to observe from a middling distance, as if, having been traumatized, he was also fading away from life. I experienced an ineffable satisfaction watching him change into some other kind of organism—something less than a man (which he always was), but without the unconscious dignity of another animal.

"No, it cannot," I told him, remembering mine. I just went round and round. Fellow didn't know what to do with me. He kept on suggesting that I look to some brightly polished goal or ideal. I kept on telling him that nothing could be so bright, so all-consuming, that I could forget my central preoccupation. It was at that time that I began to have violent fantasies, though they eventually went away. When I confronted Bruce, I'd dreamt something almost idyllic, with nature prancing about, bee-loud glades humming at the tops of their voices, and maidens—true maidens—strumming on small guitars that eventually became gondolas. The only anomaly: their private parts were super-large, as if all of creation had sunk, or would sink, into them.

"Do you want money?"

"Don't insult me."

"What *do* you want?"

"I want, for one, to be away from you. For another...I suppose I want to go back to that moment when we'd done our last show and become the man I should have. That's what I want. That's what I want more than anything, and all of your money and good intentions and pouffy little blandishments cannot get it for me. Time is one thing we can never get back. But it is at the very center of my desire."

Peregrine scooted his chair back somewhat. He started to say something, but I wouldn't let him. It was my show from now on. Yet I suddenly relented, as if it was not only his turn, but he had somehow earned it. But he was still scared. I had to give him a nod to start him up again, as if he were a mechanical thing I had to set in motion.

"When I made the decision, I must admit that I didn't consider you-as-victim, if you will. I was just full of my grand design, in which you did not, alas, figure. I thought that, when you learned of it, you'd hurt for a while and move on. How were you to know how big they'd get? But, of course, they did, didn't they? Putting myself in your position..."

"You can't do that," I said ferociously.

He withdrew from the table a bit more. Someone from an adjacent area, a red and green one—the place was divided into little mood-swing compartments—looked our way. The look I returned made his expression wither. It had started out slightly annoyed; after he contemplated the look on my face, his expression collapsed and wandered between assault and recovery. He'd been in a movie I saw a while back. Played a guy with a fixation for blondes. Whom he dispatched on a regular basis. Some of their body-parts wound up in unusual places. He was said to have had a sort of breakdown after it.

"No, I suppose not," said Peregrine, looking like a man with no place to go.

"No," he repeated, lowering his voice, "I suppose—as the Americans say—you have me there."

Peregrine was about to begin a story, but thought better of it. I'm sure he'd seen people in emotional distress, but I sincerely doubt whether he saw many of them *mano-a-mano*.

"I'm sorry. Until the, uh, incident, I had no idea how much this thing has been chafing at you. I really didn't. "

I moved closer, not to establish the undesirable intimacy he still craved, but to make him as uncomfortable as proximity could.

"Why did you make such a big deal about settling my

bail?"

"Well, it was the least I could do," he said, as if I'd asked him whether his balls were made of jack-o-lanterns.

"Sure it had nothing to do with all of those sneak-thieves hanging about with their microphones?"

Peregrine had a faculty for expressing over-the-top emotions. You could have taken pictures of him in the throes of one and called it "Surprise" in capital letters and put it in a little book. On this occasion, he had chosen to pantomime "Chagrin"—the Sorrow that should have been usurped by "Anger", but was—through no fault of his own—not going to be expressed.

"I had no such intentions. I was worried for you and wanted you to get out as expeditiously as possible. If I were seen performing this office, it was nothing I had personally contrived. I'm really hurt that you would think such a thing. I really am."

With that admission, he drained his glass and poured another. I could see the blush on his face widen a bit, like a wading pool does when you dump more water into it.

How, I was thinking, might he react if he knew of my unremitting outrage, which started with my eviction and had blossomed over the past thirty-odd years? How, I was also thinking, might he believe that he would emerge from this somewhat tacky restaurant unscathed? Hubris was all it was. I'm sure he felt at least moderately invincible driving—or being driven—to this place. He could watch potential salespeople, product demonstrators, and other underlings scurry about as they managed to eke out a living in department stores, small shops, and ground-floor groceries. He could press a button and a tinted window would shield him from his driver's super-neutral gaze, which would have observed him having a nice little cocktail. Or he could flip through a secret stash of male pornography. Or he could just revel in being rich, free, and queer—and in a place whose morality was relaxing to the point of considering privileged fags off-limits to the law.

They could be bashed physically and verbally, but they could not be clapped into quod for practicing the love that dare not waggle its penis at another selfsame organ.

As if to save the both of us, a Keyster song started to play in the background. I hadn't been listening to the piped-in music, but this caught my attention. I hadn't heard it in over thirty years, when we'd tried it out at that club in Austria. It was, in fact, co-authored by me. Another sticking point. I was never credited for it. Nor had I received tuppence in royalties.

"Ahhhhh," said Peregrine, settling into the rat's nest of his memories.

"You recognize it, do you?"

"Oh, yes! It was your...their first. Also, the first single to be released in those distant climes that would eventually embrace us."

Not a bad tune—not for its time. Good beat, which Marshall and I supplied from striking things one might have found in Papua, New Guinea for all of their connection to modern times. His arbitrary choices had the savor, on record, of well-thought out paradigms. Professor types attribute a sagacity to these choices, which—if Marshall had ever read their exegeses—would have astonished the man who had made them. I can hear him denying the outlandish claims of sober-sided men with advanced degrees and inflated reputations. "Just needed to strike something that wasn't a drum. Know what I mean?"

"Good hook in that one. Don't misunderstand me. I would like to say that I anticipated its world-wide appeal, but, while I thought it was snappy enough, I was merely thrilled to have it reach the airwaves at all. Weren't we simple in those days? So very simple!"

> *Do you want me to love you now*
> *Or wait until tomorrow?*
> *(We really shouldn't wait—*
> *It could become too late)*

I know that love can lead to sorrow
So tell me
O tell me
What shall I do!

"Don't tell me you don't remember that fondly," said Peregrine, his old self coming back. The next glass had gone in and more was coming out of the bottle. With a cock of his head, he told the waiter we'd like more drink. The waiter de-materialized, as so many waiters around there seemed to do, and showed up with another bottle of the same stuff. He started to pour, but Peregrine waved him away. Upon which signal he de-materialized again.

"I would if I'd been given credit for that song."

"You?"

"Yeah. Me and Jake. We wrote it one afternoon. Inside that little chicken-coop where we rehearsed."

"That was a nasty little sty, wasn't it?"

"You didn't credit me on the record. Nothing. Bupkiss, as a little tailor on Edgeware Road used to say. From New York City by way of Mother Russia. Pogroms and all that. Just happy to be away from that stuck pig feeling people get when the bogeyman comes around."

Peregrine was now expressing "Chagrin", but with a finely shaded sensibility, like an actor who's been told to play "between emotions."

"I don't think that could be. Jake never mentioned it."

"Jake was out for Jake—as multi-talented as he undoubtedly was."

"But why would he take credit for just a little song? He and Bruce batted them out like shuttlecocks. And shared billing from the very outset."

I stared up at the ceiling, from which descended a rosette that had been made of intersecting bolts of fabric. It was quite clever in the way it pantomimed a living thing.

"Perhaps they didn't want to spoil their...Perfect. Record," I said. "Don't want nasty little Vijay on it," I said.

"With that suggestion of foreign influence. Vijay, striker of loud instruments," I said. "Not skilled or subtle enough to strum a guitar. And not independent enough to write tunes of his own," I said.

"I promise you, I never knew of that. Cross my heart. I never did."

I actually believed Peregrine on this one. Speaking of panto, he was no longer embodying certain emotions; he was feeling something and letting the words fly out of it. I felt I should stop them, however, with a few of my own.

"If I'd married and had a kid, he or she could have sailed through college on that one. And I could've had a nice little potting-shed out back. Some cucumbers maybe. Or root vegetables. Always liked root vegetables. Root vegetables are good for the digestion. When you have unsightly things in your stomach, you get sick. But root vegetables clean them all out. They're great things, root vegetables. I'd love to be able to set them on a root-sorting table—if there are any such—and bang through them all. Have one helluva slambang sorting soiree. A sorting-fest. A sorting bonanza. That's what I could've had. And may still."

"I'm sor—" Peregrine started to say before I took his collar.

"I want fucking root vegetables," I said, holding him close, "like you want to suck pussy. I want goddamned root vegetables like you sit around and dream of some sweet little lady coming in and roasting your weenie over a very slow fire, with lots of wood-smoke to it. I want motherfucking root vegetables the way you want to go back to your bloody little job at the radio station, spinning off the hits and sucking up to the manager so he'll throw a little Elvis into the mix. Or Jerry Lee. Or even those classic bounders: Jake, Bruce, Townsend, Marshall and, yes, I was still there and you were still spinning and faggots were getting the shit kicked out of them in every schoolyard in our glorious emerald isle."

The waiter materialized again.

"Something I can help you with?"

"Wish to hell you could, but I think I should let this little poofter go. He needs his breathing. Without it, he won't get to enjoy any of his perks."

With that, I exited the building.

It would be the last time I saw Peregrine before learning of his unseasonable demise. Of course, I didn't really see his face, which had gone splotchy from the tourniquet I had applied to his carotid artery. But knowing that he might not enjoy any of his "perks" for a while was quite enough.

16

I had a recurring dream about Pouffy, which speaks well of one of us, I can't say whom. In it, Pouffy and I —he's always Pouffy in the dream and not his proper name—are in a library, one of those cavernous places where leather-bound books reach, from glassed-in shelves, all the way up to a vaulted ceiling, which is, often as not, cloudy-looking from all of the dust-motes light from clerestory windows catches as they descend. Yet this particular library is roofed in clouds, great big fluffy ones such as sheep are supposed to live in. And where the Afterlife starts, as if It needs some sort of Yellow Brick Road to get there. Pouffy and I are scholarly people, sitting along an enormous table with old and forgotten tomes which we have to ask subalterns to get for us. Pouffy and I are more or less even as to book-count, and so serenely blissful in our love of learning that we look like little angels.

"Could you be a dear," asks Pouffy of somebody who never stops making her rounds, "and find me something?"

"Oh, yes," she says. "And what will that be?"

"If possible, I would like your most definitive volume on the subject of loyalty. Then I want you to bring me a similar volume on the subject of betrayal. That's what my thesis is about. *Those* two bugaboos."

With this confession, he looks over at me as if we're nursing a bottle of schnapps together. I look back at him and shrug. I clearly have more unpleasant (or esoteric) reading to do.

After the flunkey is out of earshot—assuming earshot applies to the dream-state—Pouffy manages to levitate in my direction. When he gets to me, he eases himself down so that we are as close to eye-level as a sitting man and an aerial one can be.

"I want to ask your opinion about something."

"Shoot," I say in a voice I don't recognize. There's something of the American gangster in it. And behold! I'm dressed in an outfit that says "Killer-for-hire" all over it: snappy blazer, face-obscuring hat, and dark pinstriped shirt with a loud tie. Given its incongruous touches, my outfit doesn't seem to have made up its mind about how it wishes to be perceived. Even in the dream, I long to change it.

"Do you believe that knowledge constitutes penance?"

"It could," I say, weighing in on a question gangsters rarely talk about—at least not in films.

"I have come to believe it myself. It has, in fact, influenced me more than any other idea. I would even say it takes a back seat to Original Sin—which I have tried to reject, but cannot. What can I say? It's an old favorite."

Pouffy's laughter peals out into the clouds. A hissing sound follows it, as Pouffy's laughter always reverberates in that way.

Recognizing that the hiss comes from an Anvil Chorus of disapproving librarians, Pouffy bows his head and promises not to laugh again.

"I'm waiting for an answer," says Pouffy with an insistence that was not characteristic of him in life. This dream character looks like him, but has a lot more spine.

"Hmmmm," I say, plucking my eyebrows.

"That's no answer," says Pouffy, plucking his. In this case, they all come out. For the remainder of the dream, Pouffy's face is as hairless as a marble breakfront.

"You want to know whether knowledge and repentance are one in the same?"

"Or can be. Yes, that's what I want to know."

I stroke chin and pluck eyebrows, as if to show him the tensile strength of mine, and say: "I will answer you, pending the research I clearly need to do on the subject. If I gave you an answer off the top of my head, I would not be representing the magnificence of learning, upon which all of mankind may draw for sustenance."

"I don't think I have the time for you to do that," says Pouffy.

"But I must. One cannot weigh in on such a subject with the spontaneity of an evangelist exhorting his flock. I have only the streakiest notion of what repentance may mean, not just to the scholar—who is so often away from his fellows—but to our brawling cousins, who must make up life as it comes at them. Comes at them without the certainty of any school or dogma."

Pouffy surprises me by taking my hair, which is as full as a leaf-cascade, in his hands and pulling it. "No, I must have your answer now! Now, I tell you! NOW!"

At this point in the dream, I almost always questioned whether it was a dream or not. But I couldn't wake up. When this happens, the dream's got you. As this one always got to me.

As I consult, with frenzied fingers, the books I already have, I begin to improvise: "Some people think that reading is a sort of penance," I say, turning pages. "Yes, there are those who think that book-learning is a superfluous pastime. It is these people who would see this lovely building, with its cloudy roofline, in ruins. I find even the notion of such a thing unbearable."

"Stop stalling!" Pouffy insists. Now *he* is the gangster and I'm this pursy-lipped little fellow who stands between cultural superiority and growth-oriented, monument-toppling, sky-shooting bombast.

"I believe that, when we do penance, we are cleansed by it. Therefore one might say that the process whereby we learn—which is a transformative one—is an ordeal-by-fire, the pit of snakes over which one must walk to get to the Promised Land."

At which point Pouffy breaks into a spiritual, during which he slaps his side with a tambourine while shaking his body like a stripper. As he sings, a piano levitates, Liberace-style. Once a showman, one might say, always a showman.

> *De Promised land is where we should go*
> *Not to save our bodies, but to free our souls!*
> *Jesus, He done it on 'dat fiery hill*
> *Where our mortal sins are standin' still.*
> *O Jesus, Lord, let us hold You close*
> *Until nobody wins and nobody loses.*
> *Yeah, You've got the run of heaven and hell*
> *Your guidance is clearer than any bell.*
> *You're chasin' our sins right out but good*
> *Just like Yo' Ole Daddy said you would.*
> *Yeah, you scoured them sins right outta me*
> *And I'm goin' to heaven triumphantly.*
> *Yeah, I'm going to see God in a heavenly hearse*
> *And I don't rightly care who gits 'dere first.*

Having found the rhythms of a slave culture we British put to rout long before the Americans did, Pouffy takes up a collection from a heavenly host which has rappelled down from on high and seems to have very deep pockets.

"I'm waiting," says Pouffy, with an immature petulance that, among gangsters, causes instant mayhem. Al Capone fell into the mood with a baseball bat. A cricket bat, however lethal, would not have sufficed.

"I don't know, angel," say I. "Such a question takes

years to know and a lifetime to answer."

"Don't call me an angel," says Pouffy, "unless you want me to call you one back."

And kisses me full on the lips.

When I had that dream, I always woke up spitting. And I had it quite a lot. I just haven't been able to remember it until recently. I don't really trust dreams. They're said to contain powerful symbols and deathless archetypes. I'm of the mind, even now, that that they're a lot of drivel, a way for the psyche to relieve itself, a kind of pissing on the stairs we can do when we sleep so that we won't have to wake ourselves up to get it done.

17

*I*t would be unfair of me—I, who have sought justice by any means necessary—not to go back to that shining moment when we were all together and on the Verge of Something. We all knew it, but had no idea what combination of material and circumstances would get us there. We'd outgrown the little shed in back of Jake's parents' place, but we still liked to go there. We were already having nostalgia for something no one knew we had outgrown. Not even Peregrine himself. Or that other poofter who got me into the antique business. Not to mention the lady who would honor at least two of us with her shimmering body. (Also not to mention a sexual prowess that had come partly from a little book and partly from an imagination neither Jake nor Bruce would ever show in their writing.) How do I know of this? I've read all of the bios. All of them. Even the stupid, self-justifying tome Peregrine would eventually write himself. Its title attempted to evoke the working-class camaraderie Peregrine would never know, but longed for every day of his life. It was called *Me and the Lads From London*. On the cover he was conducting them, Bruce, Jake, Townsend, and Marshall, as if they were a small orchestra. It was accounted quite adorable: the talent scout and his protégés following along. Adorable.

"What are we doin' here again?" asked Townsend, who sat down before his guitar. He loved tuning the thing, possibly more than he enjoyed playing it. Early recordings were not stymied by internal unrest, but by Townsend's inability to go from one musical "beat" to another. How he got his chops together for that American Tour is one of the great enigmas of rock and roll. He was talented, but had no drive. The movies caught that and made a star of him. Before he died, he'd been acting in them for nearly twenty years and was esteemed a thespian of rare, if incomplete, sensibility. Strange, that such a reluctant performer would have gone quite so far. So many actors and musicians have "Look-At-Me" plastered all over all them. Townsend's willful reticence exerted a kind of perverse attraction. The more he kept away, the more vigorously he was pursued. This in spite of the fact that he had no real charisma or presence. Resistance alone gave him his entrée to an acting career no one would have ever thought he'd get. Or want. Or keep showing up for. As the saying goes, we human beings are enigmas even unto ourselves.

"Dunno. Can't keep away from it, I guess," said Marshall, assuming his position behind the drums. They'd gotten progressively bigger, like a house you add onto over the years. Originally, he'd had a snare drum, one set of cymbals, a kettly thing, and the bass, which was, in my view, his *bête noire*. Though he rarely spoke, he put his foot in his mouth by way of that big bad bass-drum. He never had any idea how lucky he was to have been a Keyster. And that was the source of his charm—at least as it was assessed by those who had no stake in it.

Then came Jake, who'd been drinking. He'd taken to the bottle, not through any urge to destroy himself—or from any of the other psychological deliriums that drive people away from satisfying work and fulfilling relationships to a seat in the dismal hinterlands of one's neighborhood tavern. Unlike serious alcoholics, he drank openly and joyously. Until he was middle-aged, he was just another party animal—a young man who enjoyed "getting tight," a genius-on-the-make with a flask in his breeches.

Rather than greet us, he went over to his guitar, slung it on him, and did a short Elvis impersonation. It didn't look like he'd planned it. He didn't wear his ducktail anymore, but had let his hair bang out, like Flapper girls from the twenties. He'd also ceased wearing blue jeans and was developing a personal style that was a cross between Edwardian *éclat* and pre-hippie eclecticism. He liked combining odd bits, like a boa and a business-suit. Where he got these things, nobody knew. But he never seemed to be at a loss for new material, of the sartorial and the artistic kind.

Since my baby left me
I went straight down to hell
And walked along old Lethe Wharf -
Or dock, I couldn't tell.
But, baby, I'm guilty
O baby I'm guilty
Baby, I'm so guilty I could die.

I said my mea culpas
And I blatted them out so well
That all I could do
Is add: "I haven't a clue
Whether to smoke Luckies or Pall Malls.
Oh, baby, I'm guilty.
Oh, baby, I'm guilty.
O baby, I'm so guilty I could die.

When he was done, he took out his own cigarette and started deep-inhaling, as if he'd just had it off with someone.

"Whaddya think, gents? Is the world ready for a guilt-trip like that? I mean, the Catholics don't have a rock and roll anthem, do they?"

"Don't think so," I said.

"No, I don't think they do either," said Jake, with an anthem-making shrug.

"Try playing it backwards," suggested Marshall, for no good reason, which was always reason enough for him.

"You'd have to play backwards on your drum-set," said Townsend.

"I think we've got the makings of a novelty tune, gents. Remember 'Nola'?"

Jake was off on another improvisation, squeezing an accordion and shaking like Elvis. His eclecticism was not confined to his outfits. He could trot it out in his music too. In those later years, when the dark angels hovered round and all the open graves in New Orleans—for which Jake had a special affection—yawned for him, he wrote a tune scholars puzzle over even today. And yet tribute bands do it all the time. When asked to ponder its meaning, one of them said: "You look into Jake's head at your peril," putting that question to rest for all time—or at least till all the guys went home and started thinking about it.

It was "Hegira In My Penile Swamp". The first verse went like this. (Unlike many esoteric things, Jake's lyrics stuck to your head like old lice.)

> *Foundling hospitals seek men of fallen grace*
> *Who stalk the rutting deer, sporting a kindly face.*
> *Come one, come all if you can stand the heat*
> *Of the weather that cushions a leper's feet.*
> *O bonny souls thrown out for kindling!*
> *O intractable wastelands that give us hope*
> *That our virtues may strangle us without a rope*
> *And sing of our testicles descending!*

Forever descending, never-ending!
Yes, forever bollocks! The parson's Yolk.

I can quote the rest, but don't have to. *Hegira*—as it is
known today—was banned in some European countries
and in all of America, except certain parts of New York
City. W. H. Auden was said to have liked it. And Paul
Simon (of all people) too.

I have not wanted in this chronicle to digress. Yet I
became such an admirer of Jake's "quips and quiddities"
that my opinion of him grew softer over the years. On one
December 31st, as we were all retiring an old year—in this
case, 1993, from a bar in the South of France—I stood up
and recited the second verse of the tune I have just
quoted. I chose his densest and most difficult language in
order to challenge and infuriate the French, who had
become, in their distant way, my admirers. I'd occasionally
go over there and attend symposia on the "Tragedies of
Success." They're an odd lot, those Frenchmen, but they
paid me well and showed me a bloody good time. It is
noteworthy, however, that they did not invite me back
after I quoted the second verse of that song.

When Jake was done, he slumped in his favorite chair,
which was padded strangely. Like a show poodle, its arm-
rests were stuffed with a kind of artificial down and puffed
out. But there was no fabric—let alone stuffing—on any
other part of the chair. From the distance of a post-post
modern era, I can only describe it as a performance art
piece looking for the third dimension.

At any rate, he slumped in his chair for a while and
then said (because no one else would chime in): "Hey,
Vichy (he called me "Vichy", after the Nazified Vichy
Republic), why don't we work on our little thing?"

"Gladly," I said.

"Yeah? You're glad about it?"

"I suppose so. "You couldn't let yourself be carried

away around Jake. He'd find some way to subvert it.

"I'd think our little song requires the detachment for which we look to the work of the Existentialists."

"I've not thought of it like that," I said, limbering up. I was the only band member who was conscious of needing some kind of warm-up before I started. Not that it mattered much. You see them at Wrigley Field and they have a Hessian quality: fine, upstanding young warriors who can take anything you throw at them. Talent is talent. I was a worker. And still am. Well, within the limitations that have been thrust upon me. Or I have willingly assumed.

"I think I've achieved a state of detachment. I'm waiting for you to pluck it away from me."

Jake pretended outrage, but in his heart of hearts, he knew what I said to be the truth. We'd written the song on the South Bank of the Thames, where you could say things looked a bit rough. We often sought inspiration in such places. You could have turned to us for rock video ideas, which we eventually helped pioneer. Did I say "we"? I withdraw the pronoun.

"You're right. You're absolutely right. This is a tune whose time has come! Shall we give it a turn round the dance-floor?"

"Why not?

Jake looked to the others, who were relaxed and waiting. Or, like Townsend, a kind of unformed lump of potential needing to be touched with a wand. Yet he'd worked hard on this song. His lead guitar, hacked out on a horrible-looking, stem-to-stern knockoff, had a startling dynamic. It got to the point before the words came out at all. He would do similar things over and over again. For such a phlegmatic personality, his achievements were not inconsiderable. If you take in a whole song, you'll find that you remember his riffs as well as the lyrics for which they were created.

Townsend started off on a jet-trail of inventive

arpeggios, which descended into a gentle strum.

Jake stopped us a good bit and sparred about with me. But that's the way it was with him. He did the same, in later years, with Bruce, whose legendary self-possession would be worn away by Jake's incessant prodding. He'd say, "I think this line of yours needs some *tara boom*, some topping-off, some tinsel." Or: "You know, your heart is in the right place. But I think your heart is needing a bit of surgery at this juncture and should not be relied upon." As Townsend and Marshall spluttered, Bruce attempted recovery with all of the upper-class, we-are-British-after-all tactics he never used when he'd been a working-class *schlub*, but couldn't help tossing, like a grenade, at Jake, who, of all the people who have ever tormented and embarrassed fellow rockers, would have cared the least.

"Let's do the whole again," said Jake, after telling me that he thought the song was good the way it was. That meant that he respected my contribution while acknowledging his own. Because of a self-absorption that would eventually alienate his son, Jake couldn't get past his own ego. Luckily, he had a talent to match. Bruce was good at the gorgeous melody that would (speaking of adhesive qualities) stick more in a woman's mind than in a man's. His was the group's only true falsetto, which he used to great advantage, but was also criticized for it. After they released their whopping, four-record *Nothing In Christ* album—which was shaped like a Celtic cross—he was roundly criticized for his "silly" high notes and gratuitous trilling. It was sometimes hard to be a Keyster. Yes, it was.

Peregrine came in, along with Jake's mum and dad. A little sister clung to this group like one of Jake's foundlings. She might have even inspired that little song.

Not averse to showing off a bit, we struck a kind of prewar pose and went into it like kamikazes.

As we traded off on verses—I sang one, Jake another—I could see, out of the corner of my eye, that we'd made the sort of impression for which one can hope, but never try. In the clubs, I'd occasionally watch people as I was banging my tambourine or singing backup with Jake or Townsend. I'd watch them attempt, first, to conceal their delight; then they'd oppose it; finally, they gave into it and were so universally charmed and captivated that their faces had no defenses left. We had stormed, we had assaulted, and we had won. Yet victory is a one-dimensional word for the kind of total captivity we were able to achieve. We'd roped them all in so completely that, if we had been more unscrupulous—or merely perverse—we could have done anything we wanted. It was too bad that we weren't on the ground floor of things—technologically speaking. We could have made videos and streamed them. We could have bypassed the record companies altogether, as people are doing—with an entrepreneurial spirit that was missing in our time—right and left nowadays. Yet, as I said earlier on, if all of these resources had been available to us, we might not have become any more than a small Internet sensation, a faux-garage bad with a few nutty notions, a flash-in-the-pan that wears itself out like a small idea that can't morph into a bigger one.

I keep saying "our." Once again, I withdraw the pronoun.

When we were done the second time, Jake did something he would have most likely done (if at all) informally, but never in a public setting. He came over to me with a mock belligerence, pretended to spar a bit, and then hugged me. I didn't know what to make of it and did not respond in kind. But as I realized that he would not vacate his position, I let my independence slide and joined him. It was one of those perfect brotherly hugs with no subtext or pip-pipping. It was two guys acknowledging a collaborative fire no single one of them could have lit so seamlessly as we had done before our small, but discerning audience. In this case, Jake would've known better than I did. It was the first time we'd done it all the way through. I wasn't as enraptured by its reception as by the fact that a song I had co-written could be so suddenly aired and, as such, part of a collective memory; an historical sidelight; a distinct creation; and a definitive moment among so many lesser ones.

"You did all right out there," said Jake to me. "You're a man to be reckoned with. A real head-high corker. Yes, me hearty, the sun hath no shine unless it shineth upon thy bosom first."

He could never be heartfelt for very long. Before sentiment could coalesce, he'd gone into what sounded like an old Harry Lauder routine. Jake's wit was widely appreciated—which was why he could take credit for the song we'd written and not worry about it.

18

Strange, that a person I hardly knew would become the sole and singularly be-laurelled victim of my wrath against Peregrine and the others. Why didn't I find Pouffy and just off him?

· Well, I thought about it, but he found those shades which have eased his adipose tissues into the dust whereof we are made. To put it bluntly, his had his heart attack (et al) before I could get to him.

It happened on one of those lovely fall days, when possibility looms large and every woman still has her maidenhead. I was walking around The Circus between shifts, full of that nameless feeling people get when they sense something in the air, something about future happiness, but can't put their fingers on it. For once, I said hello to almost everyone I passed—channeling a song Bruce wrote about something similar. Here's a bit of his lyric

> *There's hardly anything on my mind today*
> *No one to bother me, nothing to pay;*
> *I stretch my hands out in a human way*

Yes, in a very human way.

After a time, Jake was loath to put his name on such songs, but seeing their names together was a tradition, which was, as we do here in the UK, staunchly maintained. I see Peregrine behind it, but never learned how it came to be. One of the last things Bruce did was try to separate his name from a signature tune Jake probably saw in passing, but was credited with anyhow. Always, when I think of them together, I think of my own meticulously orchestrated absence. I'm a footnote in Keysters' studies, for which college credits are given. There are even a few Ph.D's who've written theses with titles like: *The Eternal Double Entendre: Multiple Meanings In Keyster Lyricism.*

I'm not kidding you. Go look it up.

It is possible that, had Jake lived longer, I would have chosen him. But his death was so satisfyingly mundane (How many other people stepped out in front of a car that year, or were hit by one looking the other way?) that I couldn't have bested it with hook or bastinado. If ever justice could be rendered as a victim could have wanted it, that was it. Yet I lost Evelyn because of it. Of her, I will speak again.

Yes, the day Obit Peregrine gave up his pudgy little ghost was full of saccharine promise and won/won/wonderful feelings. It was crisp, unseasonably warm, and full of nice people looking their very best. The world economy was staggering a bit, but London was overspending that day. The girls swung shopping bags while escorts and distant admirers watched with a self-forgiving rapacity that was by turns good-natured and alarming. Sharing that particular mode of observation, I followed some of these girls around. Discreetly, of course. I merely wanted to experience their in-the-moment, hip-swinging optimism. England has always been a grey-looking place, with its spalling façades and proper uniforms. Those candy-apple telephone booths—which have sadly vanished from the scene—reminded me of a thick-ankled spinster going out on the town, getting drunk as a lord, and asking a young man to go home with her. They were English only if you considered an Englishman (or woman) capable of rant and impulse.

I will describe that day, September 17, 2001, as a double-whammy, with a sort of fat olive in it.

There was 9/11, of course, which had left America reeling. And us too. We grieved for its victims, were horrified that extremist rancor could plan such an attack in such a place. We were used to the strewing of bodies in other parts of the world, but not in America the Brave, America the Singular—America the Exception. Jake had always been sentimental about his adopted country, giving interviews that trumpeted its uniquely "individualist" character. He even enjoyed its tropes, and without the wink/wink, nod/nod that accompanied most of his partisan feelings. I even remember him reciting America's *Pledge of Allegiance* on a talk show. People from those heady days of freewheeling protests scratched their heads that such an Iconoclast could be so sincerely patriotic. Yet, given his departure from the Keyster orbit, as well as his own absorption into American life, it was understandable. America's idolatry had made his American adventure possible, and while he would never be the musician he had been with Bruce, Townsend, and Marshall keeping him on his toes, his persona reigned triumphant and had never lost its appeal. Even those days when he "acted out" were easily assimilated. Whatever Jake did was all right. He had acquired the immunity that is the guerdon, not only of success, but of finding the heart of an entire generation and heaving himself into it. He knew something about America's brighter promises, having been allowed so many of them himself. Yet I don't think he understood its darker passion for the conformity that led to the wars that came after those planes smashed into the World Trade Center and catapulted day-workers, secretaries, and other hapless people into a clear-blue sky that looked like Peace had descended upon New York City and captured it for all time.

As I turned a corner, watching another girl, I saw Evelyn. She was walking towards me. There was nothing I could do but acknowledge her.

I don't know who saw whom first, but, when it came time to speak, we were both somewhat rattled. She decided to trot out her very best, off-the-cuff demeanor, whose sparkle settled into a frantic denial: of our past, The Past, any past at all.

"How are you?" she exclaimed, taking my hands in hers, but dropping them straightaway.

"You know. All right. You look...nice."

"I'm so old. Been taking classes. You know, for thighs and tummy."

"It shows," I said.

"You're sweet, but...what brings you here?"

"I work not far away."

"Still with, uh...?"

"Clew and Sons."

"I hear you've moved up in the ranks."

"Have you?" I said. Where would she have heard about the pecking order in an antiques business?

"Somewhere. You know. It's a smaller world than we think."

"Yes," I said. "But the trick is in sorting out the leftovers."

"I suppose that's what we are," she said, shifting her weight in the fetching manner she could still pull off. She did look good; hardly aged a bit, except around the neck. No wattles, but lesser elasticity. She was wearing a kind of pea-jacket, which made her seem fashionably overdressed. The old heels were missing, replaced by the sensible shoes of the daily jogger. She wanted to say that she was still a woman, but a practical woman who cared little for show.

"What have you been up to these days?" I asked,

dodging somebody who, like me, had probably been watching Evelyn before she assumed the conversational position.

"I've changed jobs."

"Oh?"

"Yes, I now make millionaires comfortable with their loot, though I work with moderate-income people too. With them, it's on a sliding scale. I wouldn't want to hobnob with jet-setters only."

"I see."

"If you must know, I'm a *feng shui* specialist."

I shrugged, as people do when they're out of their depth—or want to hide in their opinions. I knew vaguely what *feng shui* was. It was, first and foremost, a sort of joke. I heard about it in my line of work all the time. Clients would return a piece of furniture because it put certain "energy fields" and "complementary vibrations" out of whack. When people talk like this, there's no reasoning with them.

I'd developed a *feng shui*-resistant attitude, which consisted of agreeing with the client, but not budging in my lack of regard for his or her dependency on something an out-of-work Japanese designer invented while tossing down sakis in a Tokyo bar. Or if he or she didn't, that's the way it should have happened. I have no "beef" against man or woman cashing in on an idea—unless it's stolen— but please! *Feng shui* is another faddist preoccupation that keeps us in thrall to trivial sensations and pseudo-science. I fully understand how furnishings may create a mood, but I don't think they "vibrate" or distill energies that cause illness and disease. If they did, you'd have to insure each and every one as if they were a person with certain susceptibilities that might get caught up in "something" or fail to click when they should, or fall victim to a cancerous proliferation in which case nothing was as it seemed anymore and you might as well chuck the whole thing.

"I'm sure you don't believe in that sort of thing," she

said, as a way of reflecting on my ages-old conservatism.

"In a complicated cosmos, everything has its place."

"I should have expected you to say something so delightfully neutral. Shall we have some tea?"

"I suppose we could," I said, with that looking-at-one's-watch watchfulness.

I found myself, as we walked toward one of those tiny, tiny places that crop up on the periphery of enormous ones, growing angry with Evelyn. I'd not given myself a chance to process or assimilate our destruction, as I came to think of it. When she stormed out of our apartment, she left me no room, so to speak. I could not appeal for clemency, for I'd had none for Jake. I could not draw upon a comfortably familiar past because ours was in the developmental stage and hadn't much of that behind it. And I didn't have the courage to insist that our love was worth fighting for. Perhaps such a sentiment had appeared too often, and with a contemptible fluency, in too many pop songs. I could have fought for it had I been able to phrase it—or think about it—differently. As we entered this new and shiny place she had chosen for us—based on its superior vibrations, no doubt—I was torn between bolting out of there or becoming that steely face on the other side of a booth or table. Film directors use it all the time. It draws people into a scene even as they would wish to flee it.

"Is this all right?" she asked me of our table. (I couldn't tell whether she'd chosen the place or I had. We seemed to have struck a mutual agreement without having discuss it. For some reason, that made me angrier than before. Here was a kind of regressive intimacy that had no place to go.)

"It's fine."

"Well, then. Tell me about yourself."

I found myself reluctant to share anything with her and confined my story to the barest outlines: continuing advancement within the business, a nicer place with some trees and shrubbery, and a very sweet set of neighbors. Do anything for you: watch the house if you were on holiday, feed your cat if you had one, even water your yard if it started to look brown. I'd taken to gardening—which Townsend was doing when he fell ill. (More on that a bit later.)

"Sounds like you're very comfortable."

"In a manner of speaking. What about you?"

She let the waiter put down our tea things and solemnly regret that we would have nothing else. He flounced away as only a part-time actor can.

"Well, I was in a disastrous relationship for six years. Six long years, during which I gained fifty pounds. Can you imagine it?"

"No," I admitted. "I cannot."

"Well, when that was done, I took myself in hand and got rid of those pounds, for one thing. I'm determined to keep them off. I was just on my daily walk when we...when I ran into you."

She seemed to be suggesting that I might have been following her. I wanted to quash that notion in a trice.

"I walk here almost every day," I told her. "This one beckoned particularly."

"Yes, it is beautiful out. So strange, considering..."

"I'd rather not talk about that, if you don't mind."

She could have put milk in her tea, but did not—part of the new austerity that had melted all those pounds.

"No, I wouldn't either. I think I must have been similarly motivated. I don't walk much. If you must know, I prefer to jog."

"I was into that for a while. Got a shin-splint and had to quit."

"You look bloody marvelous," she said to me in that "I really mean it" sort of voice, which can be totally sincere.

"I'm sure you exaggerate, but I will accept the compliment and extend it to you. Back atcha, as the Americans say."

There ensued a silence, whose awkwardness began to

accumulate like negative points or rain days. Without intending to, I broached a subject I had wanted to leave out.

"After you left me," I said, "I had a hard time of it."

"I wish you wouldn't talk about that."

"Why not? It's that white elephant that people who are temporarily spared their white elephants can finally air out."

She daubed at her face with an oversized napkin. I thought she might leave, but said she was going to the loo.

"Shall I order something else?"

"I don't know if you should," she said, with a sense of wanting to conclude our interview.

"All right; I'll wait."

"That would be good."

While she was absent, I studied our fellow tea-drinkers, who had learned to wolf everything down. Gone was the stately ritual of yore, replaced by ravenous scone-eaters, competitive product consumers, and ten percent gratuity specialists. They were all younger and brighter; small in waist and conscientious in their portions. They all likely had a pair of jogging shoes somewhere and a calorie monitor and all the rest of it. One conversation, however, caught my ear.

"Nobody could touch them. While they were in their prime, they had no rivals."

"They sound so quaint today."

"They sound timeless, you mean. The quaintness is in the technology. Just vinyl records then. I've been collecting them. I've got most of their singles from the mid-sixties. Missing a few good ones. Some are just too dear."

"Why do you bother? You can just lift them off the Internet."

"You can, you may, but you shouldn't. Besides, I like the feel of an old record. You pull it out of its sleeve, feel the tired little grooves, study the label, then put the needle on. Call me old-fashioned, but I'm into the whole experience."

"Suit yourself, but I still say you're out of touch. The Keysters. They're just too comfortable, know what I mean? They're like toast with marmalade. You rely on them too much. I want discomfort. I want danger. I want the suggestion, if not the actual occurrence, of something that might blow up. Where do you find that in your precious Keyster file? I daresay nowhere. Nowhere at all."

Well, the radicals of one day become the chair-sitters of the next. Nothing to do about that. But I could do something about an idea that was forming.

Before I knew it, I was daubing my chin and going over to the table from which said conversation had originated.

"Excuse me, but I couldn't help overhearing your conversation."

"Dear lord," said the Keyster advocate. "Were we that loud?"

"I have exceptional hearing," I said, telling the absolute truth.

"Yes?" asked the other man.

"I want to ask you, sir," I said to the Keysterite, "whether you have heard of something. Hearing of your affection for the old group, you might have. Or you might not have. I'm just testing your knowledge of pop music trivia. I'm a bit of a fan myself."

"Then settle something for us. Who's the best band of that era, The Keysters or the Haverhills?"

"In my humble opinion, the former."

The Keyster guy did a small victory dance.

"Who's your daddy?" he asked his companion, repeating the phrase without guile, and without much consideration for the people around him.

His companion apologized.

"He's an insufferable winner."

"So are we all," he said. "Oh, but you had a question for us."

"Yes," I said, not drawing up a chair, but giving the

impression that I might. "Does the name Vijay Asunder mean anything to you?"

"What's that again?"

I repeated the name a bit more slowly. And noticed Evelyn sliding back into her chair. I held my "Just one moment" finger up, which she acknowledged by daubing her mouth and giving me a little nod.

"Uh...seems to ring a bell, but...no, I don't think so."

"He had something to do with...them?"

"In a small way, yes."

"I'm drawing a blank," he said to me. To his companion: "Are you?"

"I fear that the name means nothing to me. Who was he?"

"Just a supernumerary. A cipher, really. No one of any importance. Just someone you might, as a Keyster fanatic, know of."

"I'm not really a fanatic. I just like the sound. You might call me an audiophile."

"Which starts with his own voice, I would think," teased the companion.

"Very well. Thanks. I appreciate your candor."

As I walked back across the room, with its bamboo mats and Chekhov-infused waiters, I caught the two men conferring with one another privately. Unlike before, I couldn't hear their conversation.

When I returned to our table, Evelyn had assumed a harder-pressed look.

"I'm sorry, Veegee," she said to me. "I can't do this conversation. I've thought about you a great deal over the years and cherish our relationship more than I can say, but...it's still somewhat painful. I know I should be over it by this time, but, when I was with that other guy, I found myself thinking of you all alone. I mean, I didn't necessarily assume you were by yourself. You're an attractive fellow who could probably get anyone he wanted."

"I doubt that," I said, meaning it.

"What I'm trying to say is that I can't go back. It's hard enough sticking to the work I do, keeping myself away from the proverbial cookie-jar, and just rattling along. But know that I still care about you and sometimes wish we could be together. That little year we had was, as it's turned out, a very big one. Very big indeed."

With that admission, she pulled her chair back, looked toward whatever future she was thinking might be possible, and left the restaurant. She'd put down some notes—more than enough to pay for our little indulgence. When I looked over at the two younger men, they were still conferring with one another.

I paid the check, hesitated for a while at the door, and resumed my walk through a bright city that seemed to be sitting on top of the old one.

Peregrine's death overlapped this other with a kind of pre-destined irony. After taking care of some customers—and answering a question Mr. Clew had put to me earlier in the day (he liked our little colloquies)—I was walking to the station when, on a monitor nearby, I heard a television announcer give this news:

Former Keyster manager, Obit Peregrine, who had been experiencing chest-pains at a local eatery, was rushed to hospital, where he died of a massive coronary. He was sixty-seven years of age. As the nation bends its ear toward the death of a man who represented one of the final links to the Keyster legacy, it might also remember the tunes that shook the world, as journalist Beechy Putnam had put it at the time. Who could forget "A Jaunty Afternoon's Sunday", "Please, O Please Me, Dad!", and "A Cummerbund's Sandwich"? If that era had a sound, it was produced by the Keysters. If any nation had its anthem, it was a Keyster song. And if lovers at the time were at a loss for words, the Keysters handily provided them. Yet under the sure guidance of a very unlikely man, they became more than a mere singing group, but a worldwide phenomenon. More Keyster recordings were sold than any pop group in history. More than Frank Sinatra and Elvis combined. For a brief shining moment that encompassed the frantic holiday between a colder era and the false prosperity that would come to us during the Thatcher years, the Keysters were kings of the world. And even if you don't care for the political stands they took in later years, or for the careers of individual band members after the group split up, all of you have a favorite tune you enjoy singing in the shower, on the Tube, or with an earbud blasting it out wherever you happen to be in this great, jaunty afternoon of your lives. Goodbye, Obit Peregrine. You, sir, made the world a more musical place.

And so it happened. And so (as Hamlet said) am I avenged.

Yes. Somewhat. I think so. Yes. Yes. Yes.

19

*C*lew, of all people, told me about Townsend. We'd gotten to know one another pretty well. Official recognition had come to me in the form of salary increases and promotions—all because he, Clew, had been paying close, but befuddled, attention. He didn't seem to understand why I wanted to excel in the job so much, but, once he saw that I did, he showered me with the perks and privileges such an exemplary employee might care to enjoy. Ours had been a mutually beneficial relationship. I was good at selling, which he didn't much care for. I was also available at times when so many other employees— who had families and social responsibilities—were not.

The long corridor through which we were walking connected the office part of the business to its many showrooms. It was the sort of place people from these oddly opposing worlds met and conversed. Yet the younger Clew and I had never talked there. Our conferences always occurred in his office, where he could sit at his desk and I upon a chair which I moved, in circular fashion, closer and closer to it. Mine was not an assault on Power; I had begun to lose my hearing and needed all the proximity I could get.

I had just celebrated my sixty-second birthday. It was surprisingly tolerable. A cake had been wheeled in with one antic candle—created, without a sense of *double entendre*, to look like the Largest Phallus Ever To Be Plunged Into German Chocolate. As I blew it out, I saw people wondering whether I was a poofter myself. I wasn't married, my habits seemed cast in stone; and I had a slew of women friends. Little did they know that, since Evelyn, I'd opted for a kind of curious celibacy, in which I might stray into concupiscence, but was, by choice, alone.

At any rate, I let it slip one day, as people who are comfortable with other people do, that I'd had something of a career in music before learning of my true vocation.

"Is that so?" said Clew.

"In a small way, yes."

"What kind of music?" he asked me, genuinely interested. It was as if I had turned to one side and showed that half of my body was made of tin.

"Nothing you'd be interested in. It was a long time ago anyway. Besides, you might not believe me. I mean, if I told you what kind of music and with whom I made it."

He turned to this new facet and said, with an emphasis that showed *his* "tin" side, that he would be most interested indeed. He'd known me now for thirty-odd years and had taken a sincere interest in my advancement, of course, but whatever personal tidbits I tossed his way were always welcome.

"If I tell you, would you mind keeping it a secret? This is my life now. I'd rather the twain not meet."

"Of course! Of course! I think, over the years, I have been the very fount of discretion. Certainly as regards the little things we've collaborated on."

I turned to him with a gratitude that was new to me. Aside from Evelyn, I had never felt any. I realized, with a certain pang, that I should have been grateful to Mr. Clew all along. After trying me out a bit, he let me have my way.

I've reported to him as any subaltern would, but I was never made to think or believe that my contributions were not valued. If I was asked to define decency, I would have described this fellow. I didn't believe it when I first came here, but grew into it. Mr. Clew was one of those slightly dull, supremely unimaginative people who believe in what they see—even if they may wish for secret layers underneath. That is true of people in general. Perhaps there are only two kinds: people for whom unseen agendas are visible and people for whom they are not. The former are trusting; the latter, well, they are multi-layered. They may learn to trust certain people, but they are congenitally suspicious, habitually watchful, and chronically secretive. That would describe me all right. The gratitude that suddenly warmed my belly and caused a slight blush gave me a covert pleasure. I found myself wondering for a moment what my life would have been like had I known more of it.

"Yes, you have. No doubt about it."

"Would you care for the more confidential shades of my office?"

"I would prefer that, if you don't mind."

"Well, let's go there. I could use a bit of a walk. My feet...I couldn't do what you do. We all succumb to the aging process, don't we? It just creeps up on us."

He stopped to look at me for a moment—something he'd never done.

"But you...you look as fit as you did on the day you came in here. How do you do it?"

"I haven't any vicious habits."

"Nor do any of those old ladies. But look at them potter, creak, and pine," he said, pointing discreetly to a group of dowdy women who seemed to have always lurked on the periphery of things. I knew most of their names, but nothing about them personally. In some cases, I couldn't tell you anything about their jobs either. Some were processing agents and data entry specialists, as well as phone bank *conquistadoresses*. None were even remotely attractive, with their sack-like dresses, heart-shaped brooches, and over-frantic (or plainly phlegmatic) reactions to things.

I thought of the young girls whom I still lusted after, but in the discreet way of an older gentleman whom most would consider—if he chose to act on his fantasies—a "dirty old man."

"Enough to make a man lose his dignity," said Clew the Younger, who had more than a few years on me. Reminded me of a running joke on an old sitcom, in which a perennially comatose executive—son to a still-living founder—was addressed as Young Mister So-and-So.

"I mean, with a younger girl," he added. "I can't even think about such a thing. Sadly enough..."

When he turned onto his corridor, he stopped and had me bend my head toward his. In the midst of it, I felt like I was illustrating the idea of one man lending his ear to another.

"When we get in, I want to ask you something. And, of course, hear your story as well."

The big, varnish-encrusted door swung open with a familiar shudder. Almost every time it did, Clew said he should have someone come and look at it—which had, in all the time I was there, never happened. It reminded me of the firm's old age. The younger Clew had never thought of changing the preeny gold letters which spelled out his father's name and the date Clew and Sons was founded. As we entered, I was struck by how many unanticipated steps it takes to get somewhere in life. My life was, however, founded, not upon patient slogs or even hairpin turns, but by such a dramatic crook in the road that there were no steps at all, just one enormous wrenching of the mind and body, which would eventually accommodate—or learn to chafe less against—its peculiar destiny.

I sat in my place, he sat in his. All the accoutrements were the same, the air was the same, his posture—while of a more sinking quality—was the same. Whatever one might say about change, the sort of sameness I got here, day after day, month after month and so on, I found unexpectedly sustaining. When I gardened and my mind was set loose upon a stream of consciousness, I often found myself thinking of coming to work, breathing in Tradition (or something very like it), and embodying a reality that would, for the foreseeable future, endure.

"So, let me ask you, uh, are you in a personal relationship? If you don't care to answer that question, I will fully understand. I am prying into your life and you don't have to put up with it."

"No, I don't mind, but my answer will disappoint you. I fear I'm not. I see a girl now and then. She lives in an adjacent building. Gardens with me sometimes."

"Do you and she have relations?"

The question startled me, but I went ahead and answered it.

"Occasionally. No pressure. We're very considerate about that sort of thing. Or she is. Well, I am too. It's not a bad sort of arrangement at all."

"You're probably wondering why I've asked," said Clew the Younger, who opened a small drawer, but took nothing out of it.

"I will admit that personal matters are not ordinary fodder for us."

"There are people here who shall be nameless who have suggested that you...that you are of the unusual persuasion."

I let out a kind of belly-laugh one can never control or anticipate. Mr. Clew probably heard it as a low shriek, abruptly curtailed by a self-consciousness that is peculiarly my own—though I could call it The English Affliction. Clew had it himself.

"Then you are not," he said.

"No. I fear that my desires are quite conventional in that way."

He opened the drawer again, this time extracting a small brochure. I'd seen it many times. It showed various seaside resorts in dull black-and-white pictures, celebrated in the small-mouthed prose of our postwar years. Having been drawn to its knees, England did not roar back, but mounted an assault against lethargy by means of tidy ritual and fair-minded self-expression. He'd stayed in such a place as a child and liked to remember it.

"Well, it's none of my business, but I will admit to curiosity getting the better of me. I apologize for my indiscretion. We will think of it no more."

"It's perfectly all right. I don't feel spied upon."

"Good. That was my chief concern."

I had scooted my chair closely enough to see the page he had selected. The coastal village was not pristine today, but when he'd gone there as a boy, no war, no recovery, no lost empire marred the horizon past which we look, now and then, toward a future that cannot be known. Time and place are peculiar that way. Footprints that dig deep in one locale are absent from many others, somehow immunizing them from the world's troubles. I had a place like that, but rarely hearken back to it. Jake once told me about his—though I suspect he made the whole thing up. It sounded a bit Monty Python for an actual location. On the other hand, England has always been full of such oddities, so one never knows.

"So, what kind of music?"

He laughed at his own boldness. He had just apologized for an assault on my privacy and he was at it again. Every man likes to see himself as a bounder and cad—at least occasionally. This was Mr. Clew doing his cad-and-bounder thing and liking it.

"I don't believe I've ever plied you with so many personal questions. I promise I will minimize their number."

"As I said," I told this essentially dull and decent man, "I really don't mind. I don't mind at all."

Then I told him a bit about my association with the Keysters, though not how it ended. I didn't want to introduce any *Sturm und Drang* into our relationship. He saw me as a reliable person without any of the messy moodiness that is good for a story, but hell to work around. It is good for an employer—howsoever kind—to think that way about the people under him. As indeed I was. It was the only lower-order relationship that would have worked between us.

He didn't answer for a bit, though I couldn't tell why. Was he contemplating the possibility that I was delusional—something I had always feared and felt might eventually happen? Or was he mulling over the Enigma of Personality?

"I would imagine, after such a near-brush with glamour and notoriety, that your life here seems unexciting."

"I like it. I'm challenged by the work I do here."

"You are good at it. But challenged? I must admit to never being exactly challenged. Oh, after a time, it becomes a challenge to just get up in the morning and assume—by dint of willpower alone—a sense of purpose. But I have never regarded my position here—or your position—as a challenge. It's just a nice bit of a job for people who have a certain liking for deceased objects."

After discharging his last words, he looked over to me as if I might become startled. Seeing that I wasn't, I think he was a little bit let-down. Just as quiet men like to be seen as cads and bounders, they also like to be recognized for that occasional flash of unorthodoxy that would not ordinarily pass muster. Deceased objects? What a concept!

"Yes, objects can be deceased just like the people who must eventually let them go."

He didn't want to let go of his thought. I couldn't blame him. We all need our moment in the sun. In the interest of helping him into it, I came up with a little essay on the subject. As I talked, however, I found that I believed in what I was saying, like an actor who suddenly digs into his part and finds bits of himself in it.

"At the risk of sounding presumptuous, I've had that very thought. You can't help but have it after so many years of handling things that have not only passed through the hands of other people, but lost their way in the world. I mean, who thinks about an astrolabe anymore? Yet, as you know, we get them now and then. And we sell them almost as fast as they come in. If they're deceased objects, what can be said about the people who need to possess them?"

Yes, I was proud of my little rant, as it connected with the life I'd been living, but was disconnected from me to an extent my employer would never know.

"You've always had a bit of the philosopher in you. I remember when you explained the business for me. I mean its more ambiguous side. I don't mind telling you that I've thought about what you said. Long and hard I've thought about it. As we get older, we like to think that the life we've led meant something. And what you said...what you said about the underlying nature of our work, well, it cut the mustard for me. It just did. I've never thanked you for it."

"That's all right. I was just fishing for something we both knew."

"Well, that doesn't make it any less important."

I looked over to the man I had mostly seen at odd angles, being averse, as a rule, to looking at people directly. But having risked a head-on view, I saw his eyes glittering, not from any blazing insight-to-be, but from a teary recognition of something valuable.

"Well, I'm glad to have summed it up for you."

"Yes, we need some sense of purpose, possibly now more than ever," he said, looking around. Until that moment, I had not noticed that the room we were in— whose smoky contours I had appreciated and whose palliative gloom had comforted me—was so bloody big. It wasn't so much of an office as an anteroom—the sort of place where royalty might receive a valued confidant or old friend. It exuded the colossal informality I had seen, over the years, in places to which I was sent as an appraiser. Here the lord of the manor would receive me and we'd get down to business. Or in such a place I would sit and fume while some impecunious title-bearer would take his time about coming to "get" me. (When they come and get you, you know you're in for a wait—as if the thing that's promised is the thing that's least likely to occur.) It was here, in *this* room, that I had experienced the rather piddling satisfaction of being on good terms with the boss and known that this boss would be good to me. Was such a realization enough to light one's days? I fear that it was not, though I will stick to my assessment of his character. And of the satisfactory relationship we had had. Here was a good man who embodied the virtues and deficits of a world that was on the way out. And what could more exemplify such a world than "deceased objects"? Without knowing it, he had hoisted his own petard. Rather than address my gratitude, or say anything more about the philosophical implications of the poetic strain in our work, I turned the conversation back to his question.

"I would ask you, sir—and I say this with a certain trepidation—to say nothing about my...antecedents."

"I would never do that. Never. You are an old and trusted employee whose work has never been less than conscientious—though it is often first-rate. I would even say—with a certain trepidation myself—that I consider you, of all of my associates here, fairly close to being a friend. I hope you take that as a compliment."

I looked at the heavy drapes, the oversized desk, surrounded by a Victorian splendor that has become fashionable again, and felt immeasurably depressed. Within these walls, I have spent my entire adult life. At sixty-two years of age, I might be accounted a younger-looking man, but the yellow leaf has turned to sere, regardless. I could never, for example, break out of the sadly genial lifestyle I enjoy to form a small theatre company or post-menopausal rock band. I could never shatter my daily routines to the point of moving to Costa Rica—which is said to be easy on one's wallet—or some other place with whose language and folkways I was unfamiliar and would not very likely plumb if I'd decided to go there. I was who I had come to be. And if I were a kind of "default personality," I was still that person and no other.

"Strange that you would mention your association. Look at this. One of your former band-members has died."

"Show me," I asked him, standing up.

And there it was in black and white. Townsend had finally decided to lie down and never rise again. When the band broke up and he was still a viable musician, he found that he could limp along on his reputation. He made one record and gradually drifted away from the concert stage, the recording studio, even the parties upon which he made a small impression after the Keysters were no more. He was said to have produced low-budget films, but he refused to put his name on them. Merely shy as a Keyster, he had become terminally self-effacing on his own.

"May I look at this?" I asked Clew the Younger and, without my usual ceremony, vanished.

I had to be alone for a while. Rather than pop into my office, where I might be disturbed, I went to the rooftop of the building, from which an older quarter of the city, where the newspaper trade had flourished for three centuries, spread out before me, making crooked little lines in the sand of an enormous beachfront.

Townsend gone! I thought he'd never die. I thought that he would at least bear along the faded memories and the gluey snapshots. But he was too lazy to live out his fourscore-etcetera. He'd gotten fat, of course. Diabetes had led to a controversial amputation, which Bruce had attempted to stop in its tracks. He said in a self-produced advert that a vegetarian diet was the cure-all people were looking for and must begin to adopt lest our bright and beautiful cosmos shift into a shadowy place—a place whose dawning darkness paralleled the long and troubling shades our desperate ecosystem was tossing out as if *it* were its own morality tale.

Townsend was giving a lot of his money to Bruce because, as he said, "Bruce would know what to do with it. He's really down with the business side of things. And there's his impeccable morality."

More than anything else, that simple phrase was what convinced me that I could not live in a world that Bruce could occupy with such shimmering impunity. At that moment in time, I had ceased to think of anyone but myself. Not Evelyn, not the new "girl next door", and not Mr. Clew, who had done everything he could to make a transition of which he had known nothing until that day possible. I had become, in one fell swoop, the angry narcissist I had attempted, in my steady life, to eschew. And yet it had always come out, always slopped over into other relationships. Always controlled me in a way I felt to be irresistible, like a form of addiction that cannot be stopped save with daily abstinence and all sorts of strident meetings.

And it was on the roof of another building that had survived the saturation bombings that had disfigured the City of Shakespeare, Samuel Johnson, Oscar Wilde, and the Keysters that I crept into the strange and restless sleep of an amoral design. I would, with malice aforethought and in grim-reaper fashion, find Bruce—one of the world's most exemplary citizens—and kill him with the gun people rarely use here. If we'd been in the States, it might have been harder because people expect gunmen almost everywhere, though they don't do anything about them except trot them out as cautionary tales—examples of a deranged mentality which is likely to resort to gun violence. And so it goes.

I said: "It won't be long now."
That is all I said. And I was absolutely right.

20

The act itself was quite easy. I saw, I looked, and I shot. I would like to say that, upon seeing the man, I hesitated. He was the only Keyster I hardly knew; he was the best of the lot in terms of making a post-Keyster thumbprint upon a naughty world; and the void he left on the world's stage would be significant.

It is interesting, even today, how ostensibly decent folk can, as it were, pull the trigger, send the world—at least temporarily—into a chaotic condition, and be branded by that One Thing forever. All of which has happened to me. All of which I knew would happen. And all of which I've brought entirely on myself.

Before I tell of the incident, I want to indulge in a little scenario-hunting. If anyone needs a conventional explanation for an inexplicable crime, here it is: love scorned, ego shattered, selfhood eradicated.

I gave peace a chance the day before when, after coming down from the roof—which would be soaked later on that afternoon—I looked for Evelyn. If love could conquer all, it might conquer this bitter impulse, which would, as I knew, throw the world on its keyster—at least for a short while. (The world's recovery from the death of indispensable men and women comes as a brutal surprise at first, but it flattens out into an apathetic calm, which accepts what it no longer tries to understand.) I didn't necessarily want to throw trusting people and deserving institutions into a black hole, but no one in the position I was in could extract one condition and keep another. You did the thing you did and it led to a series of events, which would spawn other events and would keep on spawning, like the familiar cancer cell whose heart's desire is to kill by overpopulation.

I looked first along that stretch of The Circus where I'd first run into her. I thought I saw her once, but the girl I followed was the kind of lookalike who turns, in a movie, to face her pursuer with a combination of incredulity and disgust. I don't think she believed I was pursuing her, but I was definitely too close for comfort.

The problem with Evelyn's work was with its ubiquity. Where was a *feng shui* specialist to be found? And in a city so vastly various and confusingly large, possibilities abounded.

Her address was, of course, unlisted.

I even entertained the dreary possibility that she'd moved away. People vanish so easily now. You may track them on the computer, but disconnect it, leave by the back door, and no one will ever find you.

As I looked for her, I prepared for the other event. Bruce was going to be dedicating a kind of peace garden that had been a bomb-site for years. Rather than let someone else build something ghastly on it, he and a cadre of philanthropists had bought the property, consulted with an architect who "built green," and had a magnificent little bower made right smack in the middle of town. He would be there, he would speak, and jubilation would reign.

The gun I had had never been used. In order to inject the element of chance, I thought that I'd take it to the spot as is. If it didn't go off, I'd be thrown to the ground and arrested. And Bruce would confess that he was no doubt being spared for the work he needed to do for animal rights and the salvation of the planet. If it did, I'd be thrown to the ground, arrested, and become the target of all the ire and frustration of a bleeding cosmos. No one pretended that Bruce would ever write the Keyster-style songs for which he was known and celebrated, but they liked to go to his concerts and scream as they had forty-odd years before. Or scream for the very first time. There he was, bobbing his head the way he did, voice straining, forehead coated with a vegetable perspiration, still shaking his body somewhat like a girl and always—yes, always—the absolute center of anything he did. (That was Jake's fond, if not entirely precipitate, legacy. When the laurels passed to Bruce, he took them up eagerly enough, but not everyone saw them circling his brow quite so readily as he did.) Yet everyone had forgiven him those sweetly over-productive years during which he'd churned out the sappiest of tunes for an audience that stayed with him because he might have found the old grooves and graces. But he never did. He learned to utilize money, rally the faithful, and inspire others to make sensible, earth-friendly, animal-conscious choices. Choices that presumably resonate well beyond the moment during which you make them. Choices that could eventually create a brand-new world.

I finally saw Evelyn coming out of the restaurant we'd been to, looking fairly breathless, and on the arm of a much younger man. I knew the look on her face; from out of its well-defined planes and hollows radiated the sort of gladness I had seen, with somewhat diminishing frequency, during the year we'd been together. There was a sort of gratitude as well, as if she'd been given the second chance for which fallen man or woman yearns, but doesn't always get. I watched her jump out into the street to hail a cab, and then jump back. When her feet found the banquette, the young man steadied her with the unconscious thoughtfulness I had known with her for that brief spurt of opportunity for which one can't plan, but may well scuttle if he isn't careful.

From that moment, it was easy. From that moment, nothing else could have been possible. From that moment, I took my life somewhere else for all time.

6/1/6

CPSIA information can be obtained at www.ICGtesting.com
Printed in the USA
LVOW11s0137200516

489132LV00004B/112/P